PRAISE F

MW01075905

Here are some of the over 100,000 five star reviews left for the Dead Cold Mystery series.

"Rex Stout and Michael Connelly have spawned a protege."

AMAZON REVIEW

"So begins one damned fine read."

AMAZON REVIEW

"Mystery that's more brain than brawn."

AMAZON REVIEW

"I read so many of this genre...and ever so often I strike gold!"

AMAZON REVIEW

"This book is filled with action, intrigue, espionage, and everything else lovers of a good thriller want."

AMAZON REVIEW

LET US PREY

A DEAD COLD MYSTERY

BLAKE BANNER

RIGHTHOUSE

Copyright © 2024 by Right House

All rights reserved.

The characters and events portrayed in this ebook are fictitious. Any similarity to real persons, living or dead, is coincidental and not intended by the author.

No part of this book may be reproduced in any form or by any electronic or mechanical means, including information storage and retrieval systems, without written permission from the author, except for the use of brief quotations in a book review.

ISBN-13: 978-1-63696-004-3

ISBN-10: 1-63696-004-9

Cover design by: Damonza

Printed in the United States of America

www.righthouse.com

www.instagram.com/righthousebooks

www.facebook.com/righthousebooks

twitter.com/righthousebooks

DEAD COLD MYSTERY SERIES

ONE

EVEN THE MAD DOGS WERE PANTING IN THE SHADE, AND the Englishmen were mopping their brows and sipping G&Ts. There was a fly on my desk that I was sure had died of heat exhaustion a couple of hours earlier. Every now and then, the electric fan ruffled its wings, but that was all the movement it was capable of. The technicians who'd come in to fix the air-conditioning were too hot to work, so we were trapped in a negative spiral of heat and eventual death by dehydration.

Dehan, who had her boots on the desk and her hair tied in a knot behind her head to keep her neck cool, said, "Edgar Gonzalez, known member of the Chupa Cabra gang, shot down in a drive-by outside his parents' house on Irvine Street."

She tossed it in the "not now not ever" box. We had unofficially established the criteria for investigating a case as a) having some remote chance of being solved, and b) that the crime was not itself a positive benefit to humanity as a whole.

I said, "Clive Henderson, on holiday from California, mugged and stabbed on Commonwealth Avenue." I put it in the "maybe" pile. In this weather, a trip to California was appealing, even though the case hadn't an ice cube's chance in a supernova of ever being solved.

"So, what's the deal with you, Stone?"

Dehan was leafing through another file. I reached for one and settled back to read it. I had no intention of answering a question like that, but she persisted.

"You ever been married? You got a long string of exes? You gay? What gives? Why do I never see you with a woman?"

I made my eyebrows climb my forehead. "Why do you want to know?"

"C'mon. We're partners. I told you all about me. It's your turn."

I sighed. "Meth dealer shot outside the fish market on Food Center Drive." I threw the file in the "not now not ever" pile. It satisfied both criteria. "I was married," I said. "Seven years. It was enough."

She studied me a moment, then carried on reading. "How long ago?"

"Five years."

"Do you date?"

I sighed more loudly and said, "Yeah, I date this babe—she's a lot younger than me, but she has a filthy attitude and she's too nosy."

She chuckled, and the internal phone rang. I picked it up. "Stone."

"Good afternoon, Stone, it's the captain. Will you and Detective Dehan please come to my office?"

I hung up. "Come on, Nosy, get your butt out of that chair—the captain wants us."

We climbed the stairs, mopping sweat from our brows, and knocked on his door. He told us to go in, and we did. His window was open, letting all the warm air in.

"It's not the heat," he said as we sat down. "It's the humidity." I'd never heard anybody say that before. As I drew breath to make a wisecrack, he said, "Have you ever heard of Karl Baxter?"

I shook my head. "Nope."

Dehan echoed my shake. "No, sir."

"He's a private investigator, operates out of an office on Melrose Avenue." He pulled a face and made a "so-so" gesture with his hand. "Moderately successful because he's not too scrupulous about the kind of cases he takes. I've been looking into his background because he called me today to ask to have sight of a file on one of our cold cases."

I frowned. "Has he turned bounty hunter?"

The captain shook his head. "No, there is no reward on this case."

Dehan went straight to the point. "What's the case?"

"Stephen Springfellow. Shot to death in his apartment on 155th Street. As usual, lack of forensic evidence and witnesses led to the case going cold."

"We'll have a look at the file and have a chat with Baxter. I'd like to know why he's interested in the case."

"Precisely. Whether it's a personal interest, or a client's interest, it could shed light on the murder." He pushed a sheet of paper across the desk. I reached for it. It was Baxter's address. "Normally does 'wife watching'"—he made the quotation marks sign with his fingers—"but he has been known to track down missing persons who were trying to keep a low profile. They have somehow tended to wind up in hospital or in the river after he finds them. Not that he does the hit; he's just the finder. And gets a finder's fee."

Dehan raised an eyebrow. "A rat."

He looked at her and smiled. "Yes, Detective Dehan, but try not to beat him up or terrorize him. We need his cooperation."

She smiled back. "Who, me?"

He chuckled without much humor. "All right, Detectives, go and see what you can find out."

Back downstairs, Dehan found the file in the box. She dropped into her chair and started reading, while I stood in front of the fan.

"Stephen Springfellow, white male, thirty-two, found shot through the heart in his apartment on East 155th Street on

June 14, 2015." She pulled a happy face and glanced at me. "Recent. Makes a change. He was tied to a chair and had been badly beaten. He had his wallet in his back pocket with a hundred bucks in it, plus his credit card, ID, and driver's license. Nothing appeared to be missing from his apartment. The lock had not been forced. The neighbors heard nothing, except that the one who called it in heard two gunshots close together and reported seeing a couple of members of the Sureños gang nearby. However, she then refused to make an official statement, and in any case, it was not enough to make an arrest."

She pulled out some photographs of the crime scene and spread them on the desk. They showed a small, seedy apartment with an unmade bed, a table with three chairs around it, and a small, open-plan kitchen. Near the table, Stephen Springfellow was sprawled over the fourth chair. His ankles were tied to the chair legs, and his hands were tied behind the backrest. His face was badly bruised and swollen, and the front of his shirt was drenched and clotted with blood that was beginning to dry. You could see the dark circle of the entry wound to the right—his left—of his sternum.

I sat, pulled one of the pictures over to me, and started to examine it. Dehan was leafing through the file.

"He had previous. He was a small-time crook. Burglary, petty theft, brawls, but nothing major. Spent a couple of years in San Francisco, came back east 2014."

"Maybe he was trying for the next level, wanted to play with the big boys." I said it absently because something in the picture had caught my eye.

Dehan grunted. "Maybe. He obviously got the wrong people pissed. One slug was recovered. It was a .38."

"What does it say about the blood on the floor?"

She looked at the photograph and frowned. "Huh!" She read for a bit, then said, "Blood on the floor, about two feet in front of the victim, possibly consistent with a second victim, though no other victim was found at the apartment or in the vicinity. So they looked."

I stared at her. "*Possibly* consistent with another victim? That's what it says?"

"Yup." She tossed the file across to me and started examining the photographs.

I read again. "Nobody heard anything, except the neighbor who called it in. Saw some Sureños . . . then heard two shots close together . . ." I looked up at her. "Two shots."

She sat back. "Okay. So he decides he wants to move into the big leagues. He partners up with some tough guy, does a job that steps on the Sureños' toes. They get pissed, pay him a visit, and ice him . . ."

"Ice him? You been reading Mickey Spillane?"

"Of course. Questions: Who is this tough guy? Why did they leave Stephen but take away the second victim? Where is the second victim now?"

I leaned back. "Speculation: Did the second victim come up with the information that they were trying to beat out of Stephen?"

"So Stephen was no longer of any use. They iced him and took away victim two."

I nodded. "It's possible."

I picked up the phone and dialed. It rang twice and a voice on the other end said, "Baxter, private investigator. How may I help you?"

"Mr. Baxter, this is Detective Stone of the NYPD. You wanted to have sight of one of our files."

"Ah, Detective Stone, yes indeed. Good of you to call back. The Stephen Springfellow case."

"We would like to talk to you about that. Are you available this afternoon?"

There was a smile in his voice. "I rather imagined you would, Detective. Yes, come right on over. Six eighty Melrose Avenue, over the African hair-braiding salon."

"We'll be there in twenty minutes."

TWO

Outside, a harsh glare was added to the relentless, humid heat. The streets were practically empty, and the plane trees across the road looked depressed. My Jag, a burgundy 1964 Mark II, was like an oven. The steering wheel was almost too hot to hold. I smiled—at least we had working air-conditioning.

As we accelerated down the Bruckner Expressway, luxuriating in the cold air from the dash, I said, "The other question, Dehan, is what is the connection between Baxter's client and the victim or victims?"

"Yeah, I was making a mental list." She held up her thumb. "Client is seeking revenge. Could be a husband, wife, son, daughter, sister, brother. So we should have a look at Stephen's close relationships."

She held up her index finger. I glanced at it and was struck by the fact that it was long and slender, like a pianist's finger. "Or it could be another kind of revenge . . ."

"Professional, as of a gang, a mob . . . something of that sort."

"Yeah, or three"—she held up thumb, index, and middle finger—"Baxter's client is looking for whatever Stephen's killers were looking for. Whether that is information or an actual, physical object, we don't know. And of course, all of this applies to

Stephen's co-victim. It's possible Baxter's client has no interest whatsoever in Stephen."

"Mm-hm." I nodded. "The fact that the second victim was removed from the apartment suggests that he, or she, was of interest to the killers. How do we feel about the Sureños?"

She shrugged. "They were probably there, but then, they are everywhere. It's a bit early to say."

I had pulled off onto East 163rd and was headed west toward Morrisania.

"He won't want to tell us who his client is, and he doesn't have to. But he's ready to trade something, or he wouldn't have invited us to go see him."

Ten minutes later, I pulled up across the road from the African hairstylist. The hot air as we climbed out of the Jag was like a furnace blast. We dodged through the traffic and buzzed at the door. The door opened and we stepped into the relative cool of the lobby. An old-fashioned elevator with concertina doors carried us to the fourth floor. Baxter's was the second door down. It had a frosted glass pane with his name on it in gold letters, like in the movies. We knocked and went in. There was no gorgeous secretary, but I guess you can't have everything.

He stood as we came in and approached us smiling, with his hand stuck out.

"Karl Baxter. Thanks so much for taking the trouble to come and see me."

We shook and showed him our badges. He glanced at them as he ushered us toward two chairs across from his desk. He was no Philip Marlowe or Sam Spade, more the Continental Op. He was short, maybe five five, with balding, black hair and horn-rimmed glasses. He was perspiring, his belly was becoming a paunch, and he hadn't shaved that morning. He was nervous too, of a nervous disposition.

We sat and declined coffee. There was a fan in the corner blowing warm air around the room and occasionally ruffling the papers on his desk. When he'd finally sat down, I smiled at him and asked, "Mr. Baxter, what is your interest in the Stephen Springfellow case?"

He hesitated a moment, like he had several lies lined up and hadn't decided which one to use yet. In the end, he plumbed for, "As a matter of fact, I am writing a book on cold cases."

Dehan raised an eyebrow. "You reckon you can get a whole paragraph out of that case?"

His cheeks colored. "It has some interesting features."

"Like?"

He smiled nervously. He was obviously wishing he'd gone with one of his other lies. I offered him a tolerant smile.

"How about we start again, and this time you tell us the truth? I am not opposed in principle to letting you see the file, Mr. Baxter, but please, don't insult our intelligence." I shrugged. "And play ball with us; we'll play back."

He looked embarrassed. "I apologize. My client insists on the utmost discretion . . ."

"I understand. Can you tell us who your client is?"

"Out of the question."

"What can you tell us?"

He sighed deeply and made a big show of looking reluctant. "You may not be aware of this, Detectives, but besides Springfellow and his killer, or killers, there was somebody else in the apartment."

I looked skeptical and glanced at Dehan. She made a "yeah, right" face. "What makes you say so?"

"If you examine the photographs—refer to the ones that were published in the press—you'll see there is a patch of blood that does not belong to Springfellow."

I shrugged. "So Springfellow cut one of his attackers before they subdued him and tied him to the chair."

He smiled and blinked a few times. "No, Detective, there was somebody else in the room."

"How do you know?"

"I am not at liberty to tell you that."

Dehan sighed loudly and looked as though she was about to stand and leave. "You're blowing smoke, Baxter. We've gone to the trouble of coming here, and we are willing to cooperate with you. But you've got to do better than, 'There was somebody else in the room.' That's bullshit and you know it."

I gave him a bland smile and said, "I might express myself differently, Baxter, but my sentiments are the same. You are wasting our time and your own."

I made to stand.

"Wait."

I paused and looked at him.

"I can tell you who was there."

I sat. "You mean you know who the killer was?"

"No. I don't. I mean I can tell you who *else* was there."

"The other victim?"

"The other person who was present, besides Stephen Springfellow and his killers, was a woman. Her name was Tamara Gunthersen—Tammy. She disappeared and has never been seen or heard of again."

"And this is who your client is looking for?"

"I am not at liberty to tell you that, Detective." He shrugged and smiled. "But if you draw that conclusion, I can't stop you. Now . . . do I get to look at the file?"

I'd brought it with me, and it was sitting on my lap. I dropped it on the desk in front of him. "I made a copy for you. There isn't a lot in it. You understand that any information you uncover that is, or could be, relevant to a criminal investigation, you are obliged to share with us."

"I am aware of that, Detective."

Dehan said, "In that case, Baxter, can you tell us what Tammy was doing at Stephen's house, and what interest his killers could have had in her? Why would they remove her body, or indeed kill her, in the first place?"

He spread his hands. "I don't know. That is what I have been hired to find out. That really is all I know." He gestured with both hands at the file. "Why else would I be asking you for this file?"

I nodded. He had a point. "What else can you tell me about Tamara Gunthersen? You must know something about her."

"I can tell you she was born in San Francisco on January 5, 1993. And that really is all I can tell you for now. You have my word that as soon as I unearth any more information, you will be the first"—he gave an ingratiating smile—"perhaps the second, to know."

"We appreciate it, Baxter."

Back down in the searing glare of the afternoon sun, I climbed in behind the wheel, and Dehan put the air-con on. I fired up the engine, and we started back toward the 43rd.

"I don't know about you, Dehan, but I am having trouble visualizing this whole situation."

She nodded. "Yup, me too."

"Talk me through it."

"Okay, here is Steve the yegg . . ."

"Yegg?" I laughed. "You have been reading Mickey Spillane."

"I love Mickey Spillane. So here is Steve, a small-time yegg. He's in his apartment. Maybe Tammy is there with him, over from Frisco for some reason." I smiled at her, but she ignored me. "There is a hammering at the door, and one of them opens it. Maybe Tammy. And the boys come in. Let's say for now it's the Sureños. Maybe he burgled some place for them, or he stole something that belongs to them. Whatever the case, they either want it or they want to know where it is. Okay so far?"

"Keep shingin', shweetheart, you're doing fine."

"So they slap him around a bit. They tie him to the chair, and they lay into him. What's she doing meantime? She's crying, 'Don't hurt him, don't kill him,' yadda yadda. Then what? She's getting on the Sureños' nerves and they shoot her? They threaten him, if he doesn't talk they shoot her? Maybe she tried to protect him. Point is, for some reason they shoot her . . ." She sighed and shook her head. "But it doesn't make any sense. The report says the two shots were close together. So, what, they shot her and then shot him? Why, if they were after information that one of them had? Why kill both? Maybe they got the information and decided to kill them both, but then why take her away with them and leave him?" She stared at me through her aviators. "Shooting her doesn't make sense."

"That's the bit I'm having trouble visualizing."

"So where do we go from here?"

"We need more background. We need to carry out research."

"What kind of research?"

I looked out at the oppressive, sweltering city outside. I turned to her and grinned. "You know? San Francisco rarely rises above sixty-eight Fahrenheit, even at the height of summer."

THREE

BACK AT THE STATION, THE AIR-CON STILL WASN'T fixed. Dehan grabbed a bottle of cold water from the dispenser and set herself to doing a background check on Tamara Gunthersen. I went to have a chat with the captain.

He scowled out of the open window from his desk, and the ventilator moved his hair on its steady sweep across the room. He had his jacket slung on the back of his chair, and I could see the damp patches on his shirt under his arms.

"San Francisco, huh? How long for?"

"I wouldn't think more than a day or two at most."

He turned a smile on me that was less a smile than a malevolent leer. "This wouldn't be just an excuse, would it, John? I wouldn't mind a couple of days in the Bay myself—get away from this infernal heat!"

"No, sir, but I do think it is important to get the background on Tamara Gunthersen. At the moment, the whole case seems to revolve around her. It seems Baxter's client is trying to find out what happened to her. Her past may hold the key to what she was doing here, and why they were both killed."

"Hmmm . . . well, if you think it's essential. But just a couple of days, John, and try to keep your expenses down, will you?"

"Of course, sir."

I skipped down the stairs feeling somewhat buoyed and found Dehan at her desk, on the phone. She hung up as I sat down.

"Tamara Gunthersen has no police record. Information available on her—" She tapped at her computer and brought up the research she'd done while I was talking to the captain. "She was a homeowner; property is a house on Brooks Street, San Mateo. There is no foreclosure notice on it, so I'm guessing the mortgage was all paid up. She had a credit card, and she is listed as having defaulted on payments for the last two years. She has a bank account with First Republic that is in credit. That's what I have been able to find out so far."

"Good work."

"I also called the lab and asked them if they had taken samples of the blood on the floor. He wasn't sure, so I asked him to find out. I also asked him, if they *had*, to please analyze it and compare it with Stephen's. And if it wasn't his, to run it through the system."

"Great. Good work." I gazed out the window. The long dusk was settling outside, preparatory to a muggy, sultry evening. "We'll need to look inside her house. I'll get the captain to clear it with the San Mateo PD." I turned to face her. "Book us on the first flight out of here, Dehan. Then let's go pack."

WE TOUCHED down at San Francisco International Airport at eleven a.m. the following morning. The sun was bright, but the temperature was an agreeable sixty-eight degrees. I had rented a Mustang V8 convertible, because I like to have a good car, and we turned left out of the airport along the Bayshore Freeway, with the wind in our hair, and headed for San Mateo.

Dehan had booked us a couple of rooms at the Hillsdale Inn, which was about a mile and a half from Brooks Street, where Tamara had her house. The hotel was remarkable for being completely unremarkable, and also for having a parking lot the size of an international airport. We checked into our rooms, which were functional, and Dehan called Hank, our liaison officer at the San Mateo Police Department, which was two hundred yards away, across East Hillsdale Boulevard.

We met him in the lobby fifteen minutes later. He was big and friendly and looked as though he'd put on his even bigger brother's clothes by mistake that morning. He walked toward us with big strides and shook hands with us like he was really genuinely pleased to meet us. He shoveled his floppy blond hair out of his face and pulled an envelope from a small folder he was carrying.

"I talked to the judge yesterday evening, Dehan, and explained the situation—you were coming from New York, grounds for suspecting homicide, blah blah—and got you a search warrant for the premises. Do you need me to come along?" I drew breath to answer, but he didn't let me. "Strictly, I should, but I am happy to let you go on your own if that works for you. Obviously, if you need to damage the property in any way, dig, knock down walls, blah blah, you should call me. Or if you find anything of importance like a meth lab or a body. But if you are just going to look around . . ." He made a face and spread his hands—hands I figured were pretty full and could do without babysitting visitors from the Big Apple.

"We're fine. We'll call you if anything major shows up."

He handed me a card. "I've arranged for a locksmith to meet you there in . . ." He glanced at his watch. "Twenty minutes. You'll report back to me when you're done?"

We told him we would and made our way to the car as he strode back to his, shoveling his hair out of his face once more.

It was a short drive down East Hillside Boulevard and left onto South Norfolk. Brooks Street was in a quiet, residential area that couldn't have been further from the Bronx. Tamara had a cute, two-story house beyond what had probably been a nice front garden two years ago, with a crazy paved path winding through flower beds to a friendly red door by a big bow window. Today it was overgrown and running to seed.

The locksmith was there, waiting in his van. He unlocked the door for us, made us sign a piece of paper, and went on his way. We stepped inside.

There was a pile of mail behind the door. Dehan hunkered down to gather it up. The place smelled musty and unlived-in. The drapes were drawn, and there was only a filtering of light to alleviate the gloom. To the right of the door, a flight of stairs rose to an upper floor. To the left, there was an open-plan living room, dining area, and a kitchen, separated by a breakfast bar. There was a sofa and two chairs arranged around a TV. A framed photograph of a very pretty young girl with a middle-aged man and woman stood on a small bookcase that held mainly DVDs and CDs. The books were Carlos Castaneda's Don Juan trilogy, three books by Stanislavski, *Norma Jean* by Fred Lawrence Guiles, and three self-help books by authors I had never heard of: *Dream Yourself Happy*, *It's Not Your Fault*, and *Rebirth in Life: A Guide to Rebecoming*. There was also a scrapbook in which she had pasted reviews of plays she had been in.

As I was reading through them, I became aware of the hum of the fridge. There was a table lamp nearby, and I reached out and switched it on. It cast a dull, amber glow. Dehan was at the table leafing through the mail and turned to look at me. I stood, went to the kitchen, and opened the fridge. It was full of rotting, moldy cheese and vegetables. I closed it and leaned on the breakfast bar to look at Dehan.

She said, "There's been enough money in her bank to cover her electricity bills, which must have been minimal. But more important than that, she was intending to come home. She was not planning on staying in New York, or on disappearing. If she had been, she would have cleaned out her account and disconnected the electricity."

I nodded. "What have you got there?"

"Not much. A few bills, invoices. But this could be useful. It seems she's an actress; this is a letter from her agent, Philip Shaw."

I frowned. "I didn't think anybody wrote letters anymore."

"These are statements. Maybe she wanted hard copies." She glanced at me and smiled. "Maybe her agent is a dinosaur."

"There are a few of us left. We'd better go and have a talk with him."

We had a look upstairs. There were still clothes in her closet and her dresser. They were of a surprising variety, from torn jeans and sweatshirts to elegant ball gowns and cocktail dresses, from the demure to the downright outrageous. Dehan raised an eyebrow at them. "I guess an actress needs all this."

"Most women," I said, with the air of one who knew, "like to dress differently for different occasions. They don't wear the same jeans and boots day in, day out."

"Like you'd know."

She had a dressing table with lots of makeup, and in the bathroom, her toothbrush was gone, but most of her toiletries were still there. Dehan sat on the end of the bed and scrunched up her face.

"So here is an actress, living in a nice house in the Bay Area. She has an agent, and she is obviously working because she has money in the bank and she's keeping this house on her own. One day she ups and goes to New York, but not just New York—the Bronx. She is not planning to stay there; she is planning to come back soon, so it's just a visit. While she's there, she visits this loser, Stephen Springfellow, the Sureños show up, beat seven bales of shit out of him, and then shoot them both. They leave him dead where he is on the chair, and take her body away with them."

I was leaning on the bathroom doorjamb listening to her. "Doesn't make a lot of sense. We need to know why she went to New York."

"Maybe she got a gig there and that's how she met Stephen . . ." But even as she said it, she was looking unconvinced. "He doesn't strike me as the theatergoing type. I think they met here."

There was something nagging at the back of my mind. "Didn't the file say Stephen had been living in San Francisco?"

She nodded. "Yeah, for a couple of years. Then went back east in 2014. They could have met here."

"So maybe she went back for some kind of reconciliation."

"Why suddenly? What happened to make her suddenly want to go out east and meet up with him?"

"We need to talk to her agent."

FOUR

The Philip Shaw Agency was on Pine Street in the Nob Hill district. We found a parking space just outside the Inter-Continental Hotel and walked the short distance through the gentle sunshine to the agency. It was on the top floor of an elegant, early twentieth-century, three-story building. There was no reception area and no elevator. So we climbed the blue-carpeted stairs to the top floor, knocked, and went in without waiting for a reply.

There was a bright, efficient-looking woman of fifty with permed hair sitting behind a desk. She smiled at us as though she really was pleased to see us. Maybe it was a San Francisco thing.

"Hello," she said, without affectation.

I smiled back and said, "We'd like to see Mr. Shaw. We haven't got an appointment, but it is urgent." I showed her my badge. "I am Detective Stone, and this is Detective Dehan."

She looked at the badges with interest. "New York . . ."

She got up and went through a door into what was obviously Shaw's office. She came out a moment later and said, "Mr. Shaw will see you now, Detectives."

I don't know what I expected, but he wasn't it. He was very tall, maybe six three or four, and shaped roughly like an inverted

S, with his knees slightly bent and his back slightly hunched, as though his body was too long for his muscles to hold him upright. His feet were huge and so were his hands, one of which he held out now as he strode toward us, while he used the other to sweep a mop of unkempt hair out of his face. Maybe that was a San Francisco thing too.

"Detectives, I have very little time." He said it with a big smile, as if he'd meant to say, "What a pleasure to meet you," but got his lines mixed up. "You're a long way from home. What can I do for you?"

I smiled. "Yeah, the local PD know we're here, and they're cooperating with us. We are just looking into some background, and we wanted to ask you about a client of yours from about two years back."

He gestured me to a chair and pulled up another for Dehan. Then he kind of folded himself up into his own on the other side of the desk, frowning as though he really was interested.

"Two years back?"

"Tammy Gunthersen."

His eyebrows shot up. "Tammy? What has she got herself into? *Gorgeous* girl! *Gorgeous!* Adorable personality. Could have been a big star. But a bit too wild in the wrong ways, and too eager for the quick solution. Talented, *very* talented. Lovely girl. But I haven't seen her for . . . well . . . yes, two years would be about right."

Dehan was watching him with a small frown on her face. "Can you think of any reason why she would have gone to New York?"

He looked blank and shook his head. "None whatsoever. One day she just stopped calling, stopped answering my messages, and I never heard from her again."

I scratched my chin. "She doesn't seem to have been short of money. Did she get plenty of work?"

Shaw nodded and spread his hands, like he was about to explain a difficult lesson to a class. "In many ways, Tammy was the perfect client. She was *always* willing to work. She'd take the good jobs with the bad jobs and always put in one hundred percent. Plus, she was gorgeous and had a charming personality, so people always wanted her back. But of course that meant doing *all* kinds of work, from small ads for local channels, to local theater groups and . . ." He made a reluctant face. ". . . 'gigs,' what we call 'gigs.'"

Dehan scowled. "What are gigs?"

"Gigs come in all shapes and sizes, and believe me, I will not touch the more unsavory ones! But often they can be lifesavers for young actors, the difference between paying the rent and being out on the streets." He hunched his shoulders and nodded several times. "So, it can be some kind of living theater: a guy is having a big party, and he wants some gangsters to break in with guns and he single-handedly defeats them. Then it is all revealed as a play. Or a fight breaks out between two female guests and they start fighting, but using spectacular, choreographed kung fu. You get the kind of thing. That's at the high end."

"And at the low end?" I asked.

"Mainly guys acting out their fantasies. They go to a bar, and a gorgeous girl comes in and picks them up. Where it goes from there is up to the girl. I am not a pimp. A visiting businessman wants a beautiful woman on his arm, but he'd rather a talented actress who can hold a conversation than some bimbo whose whole repertoire is giggle and fuck."

Dehan asked, "And Tammy did a lot of gigs?"

He made a "so-so" face. "She had pretty regular work at the Melpomene Theater on Jones Street. Mainly experimental, highbrow stuff, but she was popular and she was getting lots of work with them. Then she would supplement her income with the occasional gig."

I asked the question that was begging to get asked. "I know it's a long time, Mr. Shaw, but can you remember what the last job you gave her was?"

He thought for a moment, knitting together his big eyebrows.

"As a matter of fact, I can. Partly because I never saw her again, and partly because it was quite some gig."

Dehan narrowed her eyes. "Yeah? How so?"

He glanced at his filing cabinet, bit his lip for a second, and muttered, "Let me see . . ." Then he rattled at his computer for a moment. He clicked his mouse a few times and then smiled.

"Mr. G. Sanders. He was interviewing actresses for a very special gig. It was for a party at a millionaire's house, and he was going to put on an impromptu show in honor of his host. He was paying two hundred bucks a night for ten days, plus expenses. A few girls auditioned, but she got the job. He paid up front, and that was the last I ever heard from her." He frowned. "So, is she in trouble? Is there anything I can do to help her? Does she need a lawyer?"

I shook my head. "There is nothing you can do to help her, Mr. Shaw. It seems that shortly after she got that job, she went to New York. We don't know why. But once there, we have reason to believe she was murdered."

All the color drained from his face, and he dropped back in his chair. "Oh, no. No, poor Tammy. Oh, no . . ."

"I'm sorry, Mr. Shaw." I watched the tears spring into his eyes. "Were you close?"

He spread his hands. "Why do these things happen? We were family. We're all family. The actors, they come and go, they do stupid things, mostly, but we stay in touch. We're a family. Poor Tammy. She didn't deserve that."

"Do you know of any friends or family she had in the Bronx?"

"No, she was alone. She had her parents, but they died when she was nineteen, left her the house. Why do these things happen?"

I sighed. "We won't keep you much longer, Mr. Shaw. Have you got an address for Mr. Sanders?"

He seemed to come out of a dream or a reminiscence. "Yeah, sure." He looked at his computer screen. "He was at a hotel—the Hyatt Regency, on Drumm Street."

I made a note and stood. Dehan stood too, but as she did, she asked, "What about at the theater company, the Melpomene—did she have any special friends there?"

He thought a moment. "Yes, there was a girl she was close to. Gloria. She was friends with Gloria. She might be able to tell you something."

We asked him if he had some photographs of her we could use. He gave us a couple. We thanked him and left.

Back in the street, I stopped and stared around me. My stomach was reminding me I had missed lunch. I turned to Dehan.

She stared me straight in the eye and said, "You look like you need a sandwich and a beer, Sensei. You haven't eaten since seven o'clock this morning. You can't do that to your body. It's not right. You know what?" She started to cross the road, and I followed her. "Your body is the temple of your spirit. You have to care for it. I read that somewhere."

I climbed in the car. "Okay, Carmen, you're hungry. I drive you too hard. I hear you. Let's play tourist for an hour or two."

We took Bush Street down to the Embarcadero and sat outside at Carmen's Restaurant on Pier 40. We ordered two beers, crispy calamari, and two burgers. When the waitress went away to get them, I rubbed my face and, for a moment, had a hankering for a Camel cigarette.

"So, let's revisit your analysis back in the house. An actress, living in a nice house in the Bay Area, she has an agent, she is working because she has money in the bank and is running the house on her own. One day she ups and goes to New York, specifically the Bronx. She's not planning on staying there, she's planning to come back soon. It's just a visit. While she's there, she visits loser Stephen Springfellow. The Sureños show up, beat seven bales of shit out of him, and then shoot them both. They leave him dead where he is on the chair and take her body away with them. But now let's add to that. Just before she goes to New York, she is given an exceptionally well-paid job by G. Sanders, whose address is a five-star hotel. The job lasts a week and involves putting on a show at a millionaire's party. Questions: What was she doing for the nine days that were not party days? What was so special about this gig that he was prepared to pay her that well?"

The waitress brought our beers, and Dehan pulled off half of hers and wiped her mouth on the back of her wrist.

"We need to find G. Sanders. But my bet is he won't be very communicative, even if we find him. The person who is going to give us—*me*—the lowdown is Gloria, at the Melpomene Theater."

I nodded. "Reckon you're right at that, Carmensita."

FIVE

We ate our late luncheon, and as the sun slipped toward what should have been a lazy late afternoon, we slipped back into the Mustang and made our way up through the color and bustle of Market Street to Jones Street, by way of Leavenworth.

The Melpomene was a club with a theater in it, rather than an actual theater. It was open, but there was nobody there save the barman, who was polishing glasses behind the bar. The place was dimly lit and smelled vaguely of stale beer and furniture polish. There were forty or fifty tables, each with a small red lantern, ranged around a stage that was painted black and had black curtains drawn across it. Every now and then the curtain moved, and there was a sound of feet on floorboards and furniture being dragged around.

Dehan leaned on the bar, and the barman, who sounded South African or Australian, said, "Whadlit be?"

"I need to talk to Gloria. She in?"

"They're setting up for the show. Through that door. Don't know how popular you'll be if you go back there right now though."

"It's okay. I've never been popular. It unsettles my stomach."

I followed her through the door into a maze of narrow, ill-lit passages carpeted in what used to be gray but was now just dirty. We heard voices, climbed a couple of steps, and found ourselves looking out onto the stage. Two young men who looked as though they needed to eat were arguing in hushed hisses with a girl who looked as though she could take them both with one hand tied behind her back.

Dehan sighed and said, "Is one of you Gloria?"

They all turned to look but said nothing for a moment. Dehan was about to repeat the question when the girl pointed and said, "In her dressing room."

"Where?"

"Right at the intersection. Second door on your right." As we turned to go, she called, "Say." Dehan turned back. The girl was smiling. "You free later?"

Dehan nodded. "Yeah. And I plan to stay that way."

I followed her to the intersection and then down to the right.

"You really need to do something about your attitude. The girl was just being nice."

We came to the door, and she knocked.

"Come!"

When we opened the door, Gloria was naked. She had her back to us because she was sitting at her dressing table putting on makeup. But her reflection was just as naked as she was, and that was facing us. Her reflection smiled brightly.

"Hello!"

Dehan blinked and smiled back. "Are you Gloria?"

"Sure!" She made it sound like, "Why not? We can be anything we want to be!" We stepped in and I closed the door. She was still smiling and looking expectantly at our reflections. I left Dehan to it and watched Gloria's face in the mirror. She was pretty. She had a nice face.

"Were you friends with Tammy Gunthersen?"

She turned on her stool and stared at Dehan, then at me.

"Why yes, and I still am. Are you friends of hers? I haven't seen her for ages."

Dehan did a funny little sideways twitch of the head and said, "You haven't seen her for two years. May we sit down, Gloria?"

Now Gloria looked worried. "Well, sure, but who are you?"

Dehan pulled out her badge. "We are police officers. My name is Carmen Dehan, and this is my partner, John Stone. Tammy has gone missing, Gloria. We don't know for sure, but there is reason to believe that she might have been hurt . . . or worse. We really need your help."

Gloria had put both her hands to her mouth and was staring at Dehan without saying a word. She looked genuinely distressed. Dehan waited a moment, then, with a small, coaxing nod, asked, "Will you help us, Gloria?"

"Well, *of course!* Poor Tammy! What happened? How can I help? Just tell me how."

Dehan pulled up a chair and sat right in front of her, mere inches away. I removed a bundle of clothes and sat in a chair in the corner, crossed my legs, and watched Dehan with interest. This was the girl nobody could stand at the precinct because she had such a bad attitude. Now she was leaning forward, looking earnestly into Gloria's eyes.

"Do you remember the last time you saw Tammy?"

Gloria's eyes became abstracted. "Let me see . . . two years ago, we were doing *A Woman for All Seasons* . . ." Her face lit up. "Well, sure! She was real excited. She told me she'd been offered a part that was going to change her life. I asked her what it was, but she said she couldn't tell me just then, because it was a secret." She grew confidential, as though she were sharing a secret with Dehan. "She said she had met a wonderful man—he was a millionaire, or a multimillionaire, and he was going to change her life forever."

"Did she mention his name?"

"Well, I asked, as you can imagine. I was dying with curiosity! She said all of that would have to remain a secret, but when I next saw her she would be driving a Rolls-Royce!"

"Was she working here at the time?"

She shook her head. "No, we went out for drinks. A girls' night out."

"Where was she working? Did she mention that?"

She thought for a moment and sighed. "No. She said she had a great gig. She was being paid big bucks to put on some kind of show for a multimillionaire. I asked her if it was the same guy, and she said no, but I kind of figured it was. It was too much of a coincidence, know what I mean?"

Dehan made a conspiratorial face, narrowed her eyes, and smiled. "Sure! She's met a multimillionaire, and she's doing a gig for a multimillionaire. No-brainer, right?"

Gloria laughed and laid her hand on Dehan's arm. "Right! That's what *I* thought!"

"So you think she was having an affair with this guy, the millionaire?"

"Well, at first I did, but then she tells me she's going back to see her ex!"

"Her ex?"

"Some loser she was with for a couple of years. He was an asshole, always sleeping around and treating her bad. So she sent him packing back to New York. But you know how it is—she always missed him. Why do we always fall in love with bad guys?" She turned to me. "No offense." She turned back to Dehan. "Anyways, she says she's called him and she's going to go and see him. He says he misses her and he wants her back. Says he's changed, there's no more sleeping around and now he's going to treat her right—yuh, right! Like we would believe that! Whatever! She said she was going to go see him."

"In New York?"

"Yeah. That's where he lived."

"This guy have a name?"

She puffed out her cheeks and blew. "Pffff . . . one of those boring names."

Dehan smiled. "A boring name?"

"You know, normal, like John." Again she looked at me. "No offense." I winked at her, and she turned back to Dehan. "Bob, Steve . . . It might have been Steve."

"Did she ever mention the name Sanders to you, Gloria? G. Sanders?"

She sighed and shook her head. "I don't think so, but it *was* two years ago. All I know is that she was really excited because she'd got this part to play, and it was going to make her really successful and rich. And her ex had asked her to get back with him. We met for a girls' night out, and I never seen her again. I figured she'd got rich and forgotten all about me. You sure that's not what happened?"

Dehan smiled at her. It was a sad smile. "Pretty sure, Gloria."

We left her looking sad and naked on her stool, with all her makeup and her reflection behind her.

We stepped out into the street. Evening was tingeing the air. Headlamps and streetlamps were coming on. I rested my ass against the trunk of the Mustang and looked down the hill. Dehan stood in front of me and leaned against the lamppost.

I sighed. "We have two, maybe three key people here." I lifted my hands and looked at them, like I was positioning pieces on a board. "We've got Steve. He can't help us because he's dead, and in any case, I don't get the feeling he knew anything until it was too late. Tammy told Gloria Steve had asked her to go back with him, but I don't believe that. It sounds to me like Tammy was making all the running. She was the one who was suddenly excited and talking crazy, making plans."

Dehan nodded. "I agree. So the question is, what happened to make her excited?"

"What happened was the two other people, Mr. G. Sanders and the mystery millionaire. The mystery millionaire can't help us because right now we have no idea who he is, and we have no immediate way of finding out. Which leaves us Mr. G. Sanders." I paused, staring at Dehan's face. She stared back. It was something we did sometimes to help us think. "And when you think about it," I said after a moment, "everything starts with Mr. G. Sanders."

"Yup. So we need to go and talk to the Hyatt Regency."

I scowled. "They will not be cooperative." I opened the door and got in. "Let's go prod them, see what they do."

She got in next to me. "Then I want to eat, overlooking the Bay. What was that place we ate at when we were on the Nelson Hernandez case?"

I smiled and fired up the big V8. "The Epic Steakhouse."

As I pulled out into the traffic, she said, with a kind of casual air, "I think an epic steak might just inspire us. What do you think?"

"I think we are going to go and poke the security manager at the Hyatt and see what he does, and after that we are going to go and have a couple of epic steaks."

"You're the man, Stone."

"I *am* the man."

SIX

WE STEPPED THROUGH THE GLASS DOORS INTO A SET from *Mad Max*—the hotel. Everything was brown and brass and seemed to be the wrong shape for what it was. It was as though Salvador Dali had designed it during his steampunk period. We eventually worked out where the reception desk was and approached it through giant spheres and cubes that turned out to be cubicles where people could sit and talk, and probably make dimensional shifts. A bank of elevators like brass bullets vaguely reminded me of a gigantic church organ.

A guy with a name tag that said *Pierre*, but who was probably called Bobby Brown, smiled at Dehan and said, "Meh ah 'elp you, mademoiselle?"

She leaned on the desk with her elbows and gave him a wink. "Yeah, we are police officers, and we would like to talk to the head of security."

He looked at her the way a man looks at a glass he thought contained fine old whiskey, only to discover it was a urine sample. He gathered his dignity about him and used the internal phone. A couple of minutes later, a man of about fifty with Navy SEAL written all over him came striding across the lobby. It is hard to stride sedately, but he managed it. His face smiled at us while his little blue eyes calibrated us.

"Don't show me your badges," he said as he took Dehan's hand in both of his. "You don't come to the Hyatt," he added, laughing and shaking my hand warmly, "to see cops flashing badges. Come to my office."

He led us through the vast space, past gigantic orbs and blocks that served no apparent purpose, to a brown door in a brown wall. He opened it and let us in. His office was not designed by anybody who had been abusing chemicals. It was Swedish functional in vinyl and aluminum.

He sat behind his desk and said, "May I see some IDs?"

We showed him our badges. He took them and examined them meticulously, then stared at us as though he had uncovered a serious crime. "You're from New York."

"We are here at the invitation of the local PD, Mr. . . . ."

"Major. Major Payne."

"Major Payne, we are investigating a homicide in New York, and one of the victims had links with San Francisco. May we . . . ?"

I gestured at the chairs opposite his desk. Dehan didn't wait for a reply. She pulled out a chair and sat. I followed suit. He handed back our badges.

"What has this to do with the Hyatt Regency?"

"We believe one of your guests may have been one of the last people to see her alive."

"And what do you want from me?"

"We would like to contact that guest."

"Out of the question."

Dehan scowled at him. "You could be harboring a criminal, Major Payne."

"In the first place," he snapped at her, like he was telling a private to drop and give him twenty, "you are outside your jurisdiction! In the second place, all you have is that you *think* our guest *might* have been one of several people who saw your victim!

Third, I have no obligation whatsoever to give you private and confidential information *unless* you have a court order!"

"All we are asking for, Major, is a little cooperation, and we will undertake to be very discreet. The guest is not at your hotel at present, as far as we are aware. The events we are talking about occurred two years ago."

"What you are asking for, Detective, is the address of one of our guests. And I am not going to give you that without a court order. If you have enough evidence to convince a judge, then he will give you that order and I will give you the information. If you haven't, he won't and neither shall I. Now, you are wasting my time, and your own. I think it is time you left. You are not welcome here."

Sometimes you come across a person in life who, if there were any natural justice in the universe, you would be allowed to smack in the mouth, drop into a turbo blender, and feed to your cat. But there is not natural justice in the universe. We have to make our own, and sometimes it doesn't work out. You just have to smile and take it.

I smiled sweetly and said, "Thanks for your time, Major. I know you did your best."

We stood and I reached for the door. Dehan hesitated and stopped. "Major, I just have one last question."

He sighed and looked at her.

She went on. "How come—when you were promoted to major—how come you didn't change your name? I mean, Captain Payne I get, but Major? Major Payne? Seriously . . . ?"

He gave her a look like a one-eyed cat licking piss off a nettle and snarled, "Get the hell out of here."

As we crossed the vast lobby back toward the door, she gave me a look that was almost frightening. "I am going to bust this son of a bitch."

"How are you going to do that, Dehan?"

"Just watch me."

When we got outside, the sky had turned crimson over the

rooftops and night was closing in from the east. As I crossed the sidewalk and opened the driver's door, she said, "Pop the trunk." I did as I was told, and she pulled out her laptop. She climbed in next to me and said, "Stay here for a bit, will you?"

She switched on the computer. I watched her a moment, then asked, "What are you doing?"

"I'm going to hack the son of a bitch."

I was surprised and my face said so. "You can do that?"

"It's not as hard as you might think." She typed for a bit, muttering, "When you're not a dinosaur. First we put the wireless card in monitor mode . . ." She typed some more. "Then I need to start airodump-ng."

"Airodumping?"

"Yeah . . . Okay!" She showed me the screen. It had gone black, and there were several columns of numbers and codes.

She squinted. "See, this one has the lowest value, so I'm going to guess that's our boy. Now I need to break the WPA2 encryption . . . and I am in his network."

"You are?"

"Yeah. I am going to lock on to his AP—" She was typing again as she spoke. "—and capture his password hash. I'll force him to reauthenticate by bumping him off his AP with a deauthenticate sent with the aireplay-ng command . . ."

"Airoreplaying?"

"Uh-huh . . ." She wasn't listening, but after a few moments, she smiled. "Okay, Stone, let's go eat. It may take a few hours, but when we get back we will have his WPA2 password and we'll be inside his network."

"What does that mean?"

She had a big, stupid grin on her face as she climbed out of the car and raised her hand to hail a cab.

"It means we can check every guest they've had for the past however many years they have been computerized." A yellow cab had pulled up in front of her.

"Oh . . ."

I locked the Mustang and followed her into the cab.

We ended up at the Osso Steakhouse—good seafood and large slabs of meat. It was about right for what we both needed. We worked our way through a couple of dishes of mussels with an ice-cold Chardonnay and then two medium-rare eight-ounce steaks with french fries and no damned salad. With that, we had a superb Convento San Francisco. We followed the steak with a cheese board, espresso, and Bushmills in a cognac glass, no ice. We didn't talk much. We just ate and drank and smiled.

Not bad for a Tuesday evening.

It was a mild, pleasant evening, and only a mile to walk back, downhill along California Street. She walked with her hands in her pockets, staring at her boots. I enjoyed looking around at one of the prettiest cities in the world.

"You know what's doing my head in, Stone?"

"Tell me."

"You'll agree that everything we have found since we've been here has pointed in one clear direction."

"Probably. What is that direction?"

"Tammy connected with G. Sanders, he made a proposition to her involving his multimillionaire friend, and she saw the opportunity of making a lot of money and winning her loser boyfriend back."

I pulled a face and nodded. "That is a fair summing up."

"What's doing my head in is, how do we get from Californian multimillionaires to Sureños in the Bronx?"

I sighed. "With any luck, Dehan, your computer is about to answer that question for us."

Ten minutes later, we climbed in the car, and Dehan opened up her laptop to check its progress. She grinned. "We're in. Let's get back to the hotel and see what we got."

SEVEN

WE BROUGHT THE LAPTOP TO MY ROOM, AND SHE SAT cross-legged with it on my bed. She rattled at the keyboard, staring at the screen. "What you got in that minibar, Sensei? Take a girl out for a meal like that, you got to round it off somehow."

I found two whiskey miniatures and emptied them into two tooth mugs. I put one on the bedside table and sat next to her on the other side of the bed. She sipped, muttered, and rattled.

"Okay, here is the list of guests for May and June 2015 . . ."

"It's going to be the last week of May. By June 14, she was already dead in New York."

She nodded. She scrolled and she sipped again. After five minutes, she shook her head. "I have been through May five times, Stone." She passed me the laptop and stood up. "You look. I'm going to have a shower."

She picked up her whiskey and walked into my bathroom. She left the door ajar, and I saw her jeans drop on the floor, followed by her shirt. I heard the water and got up to sit myself in the chair at the desk at the foot of the bed, where I could not see the bathroom door.

I also scrolled through the list five times. There was no sign of G. Sanders. I stood, stared out the window at the lights of San

Mateo, and sipped my drink. I considered the possibility that Shaw had got the name of the hotel wrong. But that wasn't credible; he had read it straight off the screen. Which left only one explanation: the client had given Shaw a false name.

Dehan stepped out of the bathroom. Her hair was wet and hanging loose, and she was buttoning up her shirt. She stared at me for a long moment.

"He gave Shaw a false name."

I nodded. I walked to the screen and pointed. "I think it's this guy right here."

She was watching me from the bathroom door. "Geronimo dos Santos, right?"

I smiled at her. "You had the same thought."

"Pseudonyms. People always use either their own initials, or one up or one down."

"Can we get any more information on him?"

"Oh yes. What do we want to know?"

She sat at the computer.

I said, "How did he pay?"

She typed, then said, "Credit card. AMEX Black."

"When did he check in?"

"May 24. Checked out June 5."

"We need some way to connect him with Tammy. Seems every step we take forward, we wind up in the same place. Let's get some sleep, Dehan. We'll brainstorm over breakfast."

"Yeah. I'm beat." She stood and drained her tooth mug. I opened the door for her, and she stood staring me in the eye for a long time.

I said, "What's on your mind?" and was surprised to hear a catch in my throat. She made a fist and gave me a gentle punch on the chest.

"G'night, Stone."

I took another whiskey from the minibar and lay on the bed staring at the laptop. I felt troubled and wasn't sure why. I was tired, but I couldn't sleep. Eventually, I got up and sat at the computer. We knew practically nothing about Tamara Gunthersen, so I decided to check what I could find in public records. It probably wouldn't be any use, but you never knew what you were going to find when you started digging, and at the very least, it might get me to sleep.

As it was, it woke me up. After half an hour of trawling through databases, I hit on something unexpected. I almost went and woke Dehan, but something held me back. Breakfast was soon enough.

Tamara Gunthersen was not born Tamara Gunthersen; she was Tamara Polachova. Which meant she either changed her name for some reason, or, more likely, she was married. I trawled a little further and found that she had married in 2011, to one Peter Gunthersen of Page Street in Friendly Acres.

And that really complicated things. Or maybe it made them more simple. I drained my glass, fell on the bed, and went to sleep.

I WAS UP and showered by six thirty and went to wake Dehan. She was already up, but her eyes looked tired. She said, "You sleep?" I made a "so-so" gesture with my head. She nodded. "Me too. What you want to do today? I was thinking about dos Santos."

I shook my head. "Let's go get breakfast in Friendly Acres."

She followed me to the elevator. "Why?"

"Because there's a nice coffee shop that opens at six, right next door to the Friendly Acres Auto Repair Shop."

She shrugged and nodded once, then spread her hands as we stepped into the elevator. I could imagine her father making exactly those gestures. She said, "Sure, why not? You should have said so."

"The Friendly Acres Auto Repair Shop belongs to Peter Gunthersen. I thought maybe we could talk to him."

"You dreamed this? God spoke to you in a dream?"

"I told you, I couldn't sleep."

We stepped out of the elevator and crossed the lobby toward a parking lot that was bathed in the cool, dark blue light of dawn.

"So Peter Gunthersen is who, her brother?"

I offered her my most smug grin, which is pretty smug. "No, Little Grasshopper, her husband. And they were never divorced."

"Yeah, well done, Stone, because the case wasn't complicated enough. It needed to get more complicated. Go you."

We turned right onto the Camino Real, headed toward Belmont, San Carlos, and Redwood City. At that time of the morning, the road was practically deserted.

"It may simplify things, Dehan."

"You don't do this before coffee, Stone. You do it after coffee." I smiled and she was quiet for a bit. Then she said, "So you're thinking the gig was just a gig, but maybe there was a promise of more well-paid work. So she contacts loser Stephen and says, 'Let's get back together, I'm going to be in the money,' and goes to New York to see him. The Sureños were on the street because the Sureños are everywhere, but jealous hubby Peter bursts in on them. Punishes and kills Stephen, shoots his wife, and then, in remorse, takes her away with him."

I shrugged. "It has a certain simple elegance to it."

"It has. Let's see how it stands up to coffee."

Peter Gunthersen's auto repair shop had a parking lot that it shared with Katy's Breakfast Bar. The sky had turned from dark blue to gray, and I was on my second coffee and croissant when Peter rolled onto the lot in his white Ford pickup. Dehan paid, and we stepped out to greet him as he climbed out of the cab of his truck.

"Good morning. Peter Gunthersen?"

"Yuh, why? Who are you?"

I showed him my badge. Dehan didn't show him hers because she was still stuffing blueberry pie into her mouth and licking her fingers.

"I'm Detective Stone, and this is my partner, Detective Dehan, from the NYPD."

"New York?" He narrowed his eyes. "Little out of your territory, ain't you?"

"We wanted to ask you about your wife."

"Tasha? Why? What do you want with Tasha?"

Dehan swallowed and frowned at the same time. "Tasha? Who's Tasha?"

He looked confused a moment, then his face cleared. "Oh, you mean . . . my *wife*, Tamara."

"Yeah, that's what I said. Who is Tasha?"

"Natasha is my partner. We've lived together for over two years now. I just think of her as my wife."

"What about Tamara?"

He puffed his cheeks and blew. "Can we go inside? I got a ton of work to do."

He unlocked the steel blind and rolled it up, walked in, and switched on the lights. Then he came back to us and rested his ass against a half-dismantled truck.

"Look, to be honest, Tammy was real cute, I mean *real* cute. The kind of chick it's hard not to fall in love with. But being blunt, she was a slut. She would sleep with anything in pants, or a skirt, if she thought it was going to get her where she wanted to be."

"And where was that?" It was Dehan.

"Hollywood. That was the one thing that drove her in life: Hollywood. She was going to Hollywood, and *nothing* was going to stop her."

"So, you're not a movie producer or a director . . . why'd she marry you?"

He shrugged. "She was young. We were both real young. We talked about moving to L.A. I guess she thought I could help her get away from her parents and move south."

I asked him, "What happened?"

"Her parents died in a car accident. She inherited the house and found this agent, Shaw. You spoken to him? Suddenly, she didn't need me anymore. So she said she wanted a divorce."

I scratched my chin. "But you're still married."

He sighed. "Yeah, it got complicated. I was crazy about her. I didn't want a divorce. I wanted her to see sense and come back to me." He gave a dry, bitter laugh. "Now I wish I had given her the damn thing. *I* ended up asking *her* for one, but she just disappeared. Anyway, back then, I really believed I could persuade her to stay with me. I was a damned asshole."

I narrowed my eyes at him. "So tell me about Stephen Springfellow."

You don't often see pure hatred on a person's face, but that was what I saw then in Peter Gunthersen's expression.

"That low-life motherfucker. What do you want to know about him?"

Dehan said, "I'm just thinking about dates. We know she was involved with him 2012 through 2013. You were married at that time."

"Yeah, we were married, but I had moved out. She was stringing me along—maybe we'd get back together, she needed to straighten out her head and decide what she wanted, all that shit. Turns out all the while she's living with that son of a bitch."

Dehan shook her head. "That's got to hurt. You must have really hated the guy."

"He was fucking my wife—what do you think?"

I changed the subject. "What do you know about Geronimo dos Santos?"

He shrugged. "Not a lot. I know he employed her to do a gig at some fancy party. She reckoned it was going to make her rich. She called me. She was begging me to give her the divorce. She said she was getting married . . . She was going out east to New York to see Stephen." He frowned. "Wait a minute . . . You guys are NYPD. What's happened?"

Dehan sucked her teeth. "Did you agree to the divorce?"

"No, not straightaway. I was mad at her."

I sighed and scratched my chin, trying to fit the pieces together in my head. "Did you follow her out to New York?"

"No. To be honest, I'd had enough of her. I was about ready to sign the papers, but I never heard from her again." He looked from me to Dehan and back again. "I think it's about time you told me why you're asking me these questions."

I studied his face carefully. He looked worried. "On the night of June 14, 2015, Stephen Springfellow was murdered, and we think Tammy was murdered with him. Her body hasn't been found yet."

His eyes flooded with tears. He crossed his arms and looked away at the gray dawn outside his garage.

"Stupid bitch." His voice broke as he said it. "Chasing fucking dreams, screwing around with every fucking dick who made her a promise. She had everything she would've needed right here at home."

He sniffed and wiped his eyes on the sleeve of his overall. I watched him a moment, then repeated my question.

"You didn't follow her to New York?"

He shook his head. "No, I didn't kill her, Detective. I was conflicted and I was confused, but I had met Tasha by then and I had already started to heal. I'm just sad because it is such a fucking waste of a person who could've been real special."

I nodded. "Okay, thanks for your help, Peter."

He moved back into the shadows of his garage, and we climbed back into the Mustang.

EIGHT

I called Hank.

"Hey, Stone, what can I do for you?"

"We're almost done, and we'll be off your turf pretty soon. Just one thing you could do for me."

"Name it. Glad to help."

"Peter Gunthersen." I gave him the address and particulars. "I'm just wondering if he has any priors. He was married to Tamara Gunthersen, formerly Polachova. Maybe there were some domestics. Also, did he, or does he, own a gun."

"You got it. Anything else?"

"No, that's it. I'll keep you in the loop."

"Thanks, pal."

I pulled onto Bay Road and headed back toward the Camino Del Rey. I put the hood down, and the wind started whipping Dehan's hair about. She reached behind her head, wound it up, and tied it in a knot.

"You want to know what my gut says, Stone?"

"Mm-hm."

"My gut says we have been building up this case into a huge mystery, because we didn't know about Peter. We had no motive, did we? That's what we were looking for. Why did they kill him?

Why did they take her body away? Motive. We had a murder with no motive, so we were running around like headless chickens looking for one. Now we have a motive. The oldest motive in the world."

"You think it's a good old-fashioned case of jealousy."

"'S what my gut tells me. He followed her up to New York, found them together, tied Steve up at gunpoint, beat him up a bit, and made her watch. Then shot them both. It's what you were suggesting before coffee. It stands up. What's wrong with it?"

"Nothing, except we have no proof."

"So if he owns a gun, or owned a gun, we check ballistics. We also need to check his credit card records, see if he traveled to New York back in June 2015."

I nodded. "Yup. Meanwhile, I want to know more about this gig. Where was it? Whose party? What is the relationship between this Geronimo dos Santos and his host? Why, Dehan, why was he at such pains to provide him with this exotic gift, and why did he give Tammy's agent a false name? Whether Peter is our killer or not, there is more to this gig than meets the eye."

I pulled onto the Camino Del Rey and began to accelerate back toward San Mateo. Dehan was watching the low buildings slide by on the broad, tree-lined avenue in the morning sunlight. While she did that, she gently thumped the door with her fist.

"I agree, but how are we going to do it?"

"Maybe dos Santos came in his own car. But I'd say chances are even that he hired a limo once he was here, to take himself and/or Tammy to the party."

"True, but to check that, we need his AMEX records. To get his AMEX records, we need a court order. To get the evidence for a court order, we need to check his AMEX records. Catch twenty-two."

I smiled. "But, Ritoo Glasshopper, hotels with the swank of the Hyatt Regency provide everything that the discerning gentleman might need, including limo hire services. If he hired a limo, chances are he did it through the hotel, whose records you so skillfully finagled."

She stared at me. I glanced at her and saw myself, duplicated, staring back at me from the lenses of her aviators. She said, "Why didn't you think of that last night?"

It was a good question. I shrugged. "I was tired and I'd had too much whiskey."

She raised an eyebrow. "You disappoint me, Sensei."

BY THE TIME we pulled into the parking lot at the hotel, it was nine o'clock, the sun was rising over the Sierras in the east, and I was ready for more coffee. I ordered some at reception to be sent up, and we rode the elevator back to my room.

Dehan pulled up the file, and I pulled up a chair next to her. She typed and clicked for a while, and finally a screen came up with an itemized list and a column of numbers down the right-hand side.

"Okay, this is his itemized bill for the week he was here."

"It'll be on the day before last."

She scrolled to June 4 and ran her finger down the list till she came to the end. "Nothing."

"Damn! Try earlier days, then."

There was a knock at the door. I opened it and a waiter wheeled in a trolley with the coffee. I tipped him and he went away. I poured out two cups and gave one to Dehan. She sipped.

She had gone back to the beginning, to the twenty-fourth, and we started going through the list, item by item. We finally found it on the fifth day. A Bentley for the evening of May 29, at six p.m.

She stared at me. "May 29? That doesn't make any sense."

I scratched my chin. "He hired her for the week from the twenty-eighth. This is her second day. So he didn't hire her for the week to rehearse her part, but . . . why? What for?"

"To do repeat performances?"

"Does it say where the car went?"

She shook her head. "But it does give the name of the company—Class Limos—and a reference number."

I made a note and drained my cup.

"We need to go and talk to them, see if they have a record of where they went. Who knows, we might get lucky and the driver might remember Tammy."

She gave a grim smile. "Well, she sure seems to have been memorable. You never know."

She closed the file and did a Google search for Class Limos.

"This looks like it—Mitten Road, right by the airport."

CLASS LIMOS WAS on an industrial estate south of the airport. We came off the freeway onto the Bayshore Highway and then turned into Mitten Road. The office was located on a large parking lot. The two Bentleys, two Rolls-Royces, three stretched Caddies, and four Jaguars made it hard to miss. We pulled in and strolled into the office.

There was a middle-aged man with a blue blazer and well-practiced smile sitting behind the desk. Dehan moved right in.

"I would like to talk to the manager."

"Then you are in luck, young lady. I *am* the manager."

She beamed and sat, and I pulled up a chair to watch.

"Oh, that is wonderful," she said. "We are planning a rather special night out, and my friend recommended you. In fact, she recommended one of your drivers, but I can't for the life of me remember his name."

He looked concerned, as though he really was genuinely concerned. "Can you remember what *car* he drove?"

"Why, yes! It was a Bentley!"

He beamed. "That narrows it down considerably."

Dehan looked relieved. "Look, I wonder if I could be a real p . . . an awful bore. My friend said your driver was absolutely perfect. It *was* two years ago, but he took her to a rather exclusive party. I have the reference number . . ."

"Oh, well, that will do just fine!" He gave a small laugh of relief. The day was saved. She told him the reference number, and he typed it into the computer.

"Oh yes, that was Robert, a very reliable driver with a beautiful car. Guaranteed to turn heads!" He winked. I wondered if he was talking about the Bentley or Robert. "In fact, he is here right now. That's him polishing his car, out there."

"May we just have a word with him? And then we'll go right ahead and book the car."

He smiled happily at us, and we stepped outside.

We crossed the lot, and as we approached Robert, he turned to look at us. I pointed at the beast.

"Nice car."

He smiled and nodded. "But I bought it instead of a house. When the car pays for itself, I get to buy the house."

"You Robert?"

"Yeah. What can I do for you?"

I pulled out one of the pictures of Tammy that her agent had given us. I said, "It was a couple of years ago, but do you happen to remember this girl?"

He looked surprised.

"Sure, that's Tammy. What's this about?"

"You knew her?"

"Yeah. She used to do the occasional gig. Lots of actors do it to keep the wolves from the door. Whenever she could, she used me as her chauffeur. I wouldn't say we were friends; we didn't hang out or anything like that." He gave an ironic laugh. "I should be so lucky! She was smoking. I tell you, the pictures don't do her justice. Man, she was something."

Dehan brought him back on task. "But you were friendly."

"Yeah. We talked. She liked to open up to me. She was cool. Real nice personality."

"So do you remember the last gig you took her to?"

He leaned against the car. "How could I forget? Not just because I never heard from her again, but what she told me in the car, and where I took her."

I smiled. "Okay, let's take it one step at a time. Where did you take her?"

He gave a lopsided grin. "No, you're right. Let's take it one step at a time. Who *are* you guys?"

I reached in my pocket and pulled out my wallet. "We are police officers from New York. We're outside our jurisdiction, but we are trying to find out what happened to Tammy. She disappeared a few days after that gig, in New York." I pulled out a twenty and handed it to him. "We would really appreciate any help you can give us."

"Sure, no problem." He took the money and slipped it in his pocket. "The gig was at Hugh Duffy's house. You know? Pacific Heights, right on the Alta Plaza park there. It's not a house. It's a palace." He noticed our blank expressions. "Hugh Duffy is like one of the richest men in the world. He's not a millionaire, he's a billionaire. Old money too. They made their stash in the gold rush. Then they invested smart, oil in Texas, silicon chips in the IT revolution . . ." He was nodding in a knowing way, with narrowed eyes and a sneaky smile. "Rich people interest me. They are my stock in trade . . ."

Dehan interrupted him. "So she was doing this gig for Hugh Duffy?"

He shook his head. "Not exactly. What she told me in the car —she used to ride up front with me, then when we were getting close to the destination, she'd climb in the back, so when we arrived I could do the whole chauffeur thing, getting out, opening the door for her. She was a scream."

I held up a hand. "What did she tell you in the car?"

"Yeah, what she told me in the car was, this guy, she thought he was Spanish or Portuguese, something like that, was paying her a packet to go to a party at Hugh Duffy's place. She said it was going to set her up for life. She was to play the part like her date had been delayed and she was waiting for him to arrive, but he never does. Meanwhile, she gets close to Duffy. Because Duffy is a widower, see? He is listed as the most eligible bachelor in San Francisco. Has been for a few years. But he never married again."

Dehan was shaking her head. "So this Spanish/Portuguese guy, he never went to the party?"

"That's what she said. She was supposed to make out like she was his plus one, but he was detained or something, and he never showed. So she could get close to Duffy."

"So it was a scam."

He looked at her with a sly grin. "Sure sounded that way to me." He held up his hands, like Pontius Pilate waiting for a hand towel. "But I'm just the driver, know what I mean?"

I nodded. "Yeah, I know what you mean. And you never heard from her again after that?"

"Not a word." He smiled fondly. "I look for her sometimes in the society papers, you know? To see if maybe she married some rich guy. I never saw her though."

I scratched my chin. "I can see why *she* would want to do that. But what was in it for this Portuguese guy?"

He shrugged. "She never told me that."

We thanked him and walked back to the car. Dehan was already on her phone looking for Hugh Duffy's number.

NINE

THE PHONE WAS ANSWERED BY A MAN WHO SOUNDED like he'd got his dignity stuck up his ass and couldn't bend at the waist to pull it out again.

"The Duffy residence."

"This is Detective John Stone of the New York Police Department. I need to speak to Mr. Duffy—urgently."

He informed me with his prolonged silence that urgent needs were unseemly, then said, "One moment, please."

It was more than one moment, and more than two, but he eventually returned and said, "Mr. Duffy will be free from twelve noon until half past twelve, if you would care to visit at that time."

I told him we would care to do that and hung up.

Robert the chauffeur had not exaggerated. Duffy's house was a palace. It looked like a medium-size hotel. It wasn't particularly elegant or beautiful, but it was big, and, situated at the very top of Pierce Street, it had views directly onto the park. Its cash value must have been astronomical. We arrived at 11:50 and rang the bell. It was opened at 11:55 by a man for whom disdain was a way of life. He gazed down upon us, even though he was shorter than both of us, and waited.

We showed him our badges.

"Detectives Stone and Dehan to see Mr. Duffy."

"You are a little early." He said it as he might have said, "You are a little dirty." "Please follow me."

We followed him across a vast, domed hall with a checkerboard floor and marble columns, down a gallery with portraits of men with ruthless eyes and big moustaches, to a huge set of walnut doors. He tapped on them and opened them with a certain amount of reverence. Then he turned to us and said, "Mr. Duffy will see you."

We stepped into a library that would not have looked out of place at a respectable university. The carpet was burgundy, the furniture was all chesterfield, and the wood was all dark mahogany. Apart from a magnificent eighteenth-century fireplace and chimney breast, the walls were all lined with bookcases from floor to ceiling. A couple had glass doors protecting the volumes. There were also a couple of stands that held single books that I assumed were of exceptional value.

Duffy was standing by the window and turned as we came in. He beamed like we were long-lost friends and strode toward us with his hand held out.

"Detectives Stone and Dehan! In which order?" He grinned as though he had said something mischievous and glanced from me to Dehan and back again. I smiled.

"I am Detective John Stone. This is my partner, Detective Carmen Dehan. We are from New York, so we are out of our jurisdiction."

"Oh, phooey! We don't need to stand on formalities here! Come! Sit! What will you drink?" He shepherded us toward the chesterfields. We sat and he remained standing. "Some sherry before luncheon? A martini?"

I smiled at Dehan. "Well, I guess we *are* out of our jurisdiction, so this is not official police business . . . I'll have a martini, thank you."

Dehan blinked at me a few times, then said, "A beer, thank you."

The small man with the big dignity was still at the door, waiting. Duffy turned on him with overwhelming enthusiasm and said, "Parks, two martinis, dry, and a Waldhaus for the lady."

Parks left with his orders, and Duffy came and joined us as though he thought that was a really exciting thing to do.

"Now, tell me. I am fascinated. What does the NYPD want with me?"

I crossed my legs and studied his face for a moment.

"I know it's a while back now, Mr. Duffy, but on May 29, 2015, you threw a party . . ."

"I'm certain I did. I throw a party on May 29 every year. You see, it's the anniversary of my fiancée's death."

I was surprised. "Oh, I am sorry to hear that."

"May 29, 2010. People wonder why I never married Sally Brown. She is the reason. I loved her to distraction. She was one of those women who, when they enter a room, the room lights up, as though the sun had emerged from behind clouds over a field of daffodils. She was radiant and had a personality to match. Always laughing, always smiling, never an angry word. Kind, compassionate . . . Need I go on?"

"No."

I was about to continue, but Dehan was frowning and asked, "Forgive me for asking, Mr. Duffy, but you celebrate the anniversary of her death?"

He laughed. "It may seem a little macabre, but it's not, I assure you. It is what she would have wanted. It is a celebration of her life, her vitality. She did not believe in death, you see. She said death was an illusion, an impossibility. So I keep her memory alive by celebrating her life on the day that she . . . passed on." He smiled. "A small act of defiance."

I nodded that I understood. "I wonder if you remember this particular party."

"What was the year again?"

"2015."

He thought for a moment, and then his face seemed to light up. "Of course! How could I forget?"

There was a tap at the door, and Parks came in with a trolley. On it was a bottle of beer, which he carefully decanted into a glass, with just the right amount of froth, and placed on the table beside Dehan's chair, muttering, "Mod'm." There was also a shaker with two martini glasses. He shook the shaker and poured out two martinis, in each of which he placed an olive. He handed us our drinks and left, leaving the trolley behind.

Dehan sipped her beer and raised an eyebrow. The eyebrow said the beer was good.

"What made that particular party especially memorable, Mr. Duffy?"

He smiled. "That was where I met the only woman who was ever able to make me love again. The only woman who has ever made me believe I might be able to be happy."

I raised my glass to him. "Here's to that. Who was this remarkable woman?"

"Tamara Gunthersen. The only woman, after Sally, who was able to touch my heart. My goodness! What a remarkable woman. She had that quality that Sally had, only perhaps more so, of being able to walk into a room and illuminate it simply with her presence. When I first saw her, on that night, it was as though the sun had taken human form and walked into my home." He gave a small laugh. "Yet it was so innocent. In spite of her enormous, magnetic presence, she was shy and uncertain. When we met, she looked like a lost child, yet with the beauty of a goddess."

I sipped my drink and frowned. "How did she come to be alone at your party, Mr. Duffy? A woman as remarkable as that . . ."

"Ah!" He raised an index finger with the air of a master chef about to reveal his pièce de résistance. "Serendipity! I had invited a rather extraordinary man who had visited me a few times because we shared an interest in antique books. Anyway, the man was a crashing bore, but one has to be polite. So I invited him to my annual party and suggested he might like to bring a guest.

"Well, as destiny would have it, the car picked her up, but he was detained. He sent her on with his excuses, saying he would be a little late, but he never showed up!"

I smiled the smile of a man of the world and observed, "Life will do that sometimes."

He was thrilled by my insight and leaned forward eagerly. "Won't it just, Detective! Well, naturally, as her host, I could hardly leave her stranded. I myself, naturally, in view of the very nature of the party, had no companion. It struck me that she and I were alone at the ball—her words, not mine—and we sort of sought refuge in each other. It was kismet."

"This is extremely good beer," Dehan observed in an apparently irrelevant departure, then added, "What happened?"

He heaved a huge sigh.

"It sounds corny, but it was truly love at first sight. We hit it off instantly. We laughed at the same things, we loved and hated the same things. She was intelligent and, believe it or not, at her age, she was erudite. She knew her Shakespeare, her Shaw . . . She was remarkable. And, for some bizarre reason known only to herself and the gods, she fell for me. We saw each other every single day for a week, and by the end of that week, we were engaged to be married. We both agreed it was the obvious, simple, natural thing to do. We were in love!"

I watched him a moment, frowning, putting the pieces together in my mind. "But . . . ?"

For some reason he looked at Dehan. "I am both immensely fortunate and deeply unlucky in love, Detective. I am fortunate because I have loved truly, with my whole self, not once, but twice in this life. But on both occasions, the gods have seen fit to take my loved one away."

He looked down at his drink with an expression of reluctance that masked a deeper pain.

"She disappeared. I had suggested to her that she move in with me. She stayed most nights anyway. And she agreed. The last day I saw her, it must have been the fifth of June, she left the house intending to collect her most basic belongings and bring them home. She never came back. She never phoned, never wrote. She just vanished into thin air."

I looked at Dehan. She was frowning. She seemed entranced by his story. She said, "Did you try to find her?"

He gave a small laugh. "Of course! I contacted all the hospitals, the police precincts. I even hired a private investigator, but to no avail. She had vanished without a trace."

We were quiet for a moment, each of us momentarily absorbed by our own thoughts. Then a sad smile of reluctant realization twisted his mouth.

"That's why you're here, isn't it? It's about Tammy."

I nodded. "I'm afraid so."

He frowned. "New York? Is she dead?"

I thought about my answer. Eventually, I said, "We have reason to believe she may have been killed, but we haven't found a body. Mr. Duffy, would you have anything of hers that might contain her DNA? A hairbrush, for example . . ."

He nodded. "Yes, I still preserve all her possessions. Would you like to take her hairbrush?"

Dehan said, "That would be helpful."

"That's fine." He rang a bell. "Does this mean you have . . ." His face went gray. ". . . *something* that you can make a comparison with?"

"There was a crime scene, Mr. Duffy, two years ago, on June 14. There was blood, but no body. We have reason to believe the blood belonged to Tamara Gunthersen."

Hope contracted on his face like a spasm. "No body?"

"No." I looked at my empty glass and sighed. "Mr. Duffy, forgive me for asking this, but you understand we have to. Did anything go missing from your house around the time that Tammy disappeared?"

He smiled and shook his head. "Of course you have to ask. It is the logical question. But the answer is no, and for a very simple reason. Everything I own belonged to her already. You can't steal what is already yours. I am not a millionaire, Detective. I am not even a multimillionaire. I am a billionaire. What more could she want in material terms?"

He had a point. There was a tap on the door. Parks stepped in and Duffy told him to go and fetch Miss Tamara's hairbrush and seal it in a plastic bag for us. Parks bowed, muttered something about "very good," and left.

Dehan had finished her beer. She placed it on the table next to her and sat forward. "What else can you tell us about the man who should have been Tamara's date that night?"

He gazed out the library window at the silent garden outside. "Geronimo dos Santos. A Jesuit priest. Very peculiar. A collector of ancient texts." He gestured at the hundreds, probably thousands of tomes he had around him. "I have a noted library, Detective. Over the last couple of hundred years, various generations of Duffys have collected many rare and valuable books. He was interested in my collection. He came to tea a couple of times. I showed him my collection. We talked about this and that . . ."

He shrugged. I made to stand.

"I don't think we need keep you any longer, Mr. Duffy. Thanks for the drink. You have been very helpful."

We all stood. He held out his hand and we shook. "If, by some miracle, you find her alive," he said, looking us both in the eye by turns, "let me know, will you? Tell her she still has a home here."

We told him we would, and we left. The hairbrush was waiting for us on a small table in the hallway. Dehan picked it up and put it in her pocket, and we stepped out into the gentle sunshine.

TEN

WE WALKED A COUPLE OF BLOCKS THROUGH PRETTY, tree-lined streets to Chouquet's, where we could sit outside and eat mussels and steaks. I figured we were not going to be in San Francisco much longer, so we should make the most of it. We sat on orange chairs in the sun and gave our orders to a smiling waitress in a long, black apron.

Dehan gazed at me through her impenetrable aviators and said, "Do you know how I would define this case?"

I smiled. "No, Dehan, I don't."

"I would define it as a mindfuck." I laughed and she raised her hand. "No, let me lay it out for you in synthesis."

"Okay."

"A Portuguese Jesuit named Geronimo—and we haven't even got started yet—employs an actress to turn up unaccompanied at Hugh Duffy's annual remembrance party for his dead fiancée. Geronimo dos Santos has auditioned and selected her with some subtle ingenuity. He has chosen a girl who is going to step, radiant, right into Sally-the-dead-fiancée's shoes."

The waitress came out with our beers, and Dehan took a long pull before carrying on.

"So at this point, we assume dos Santos and Tammy are

coconspirators planning to scam Duffy. But instead, Duffy and Tammy have a whirlwind romance, get engaged to be married, and Tammy promptly disappears, as does Geronimo dos Santos. Meanwhile . . ." She gave a small laugh and shook her head. "Tammy is on the phone begging her estranged husband in Friendly Acres to give her a divorce, *either* so she can marry the billionaire she is engaged to, *or* so she can marry her loser ex-boyfriend in the Bronx!"

She stared at me, and I nodded. She continued.

"Next thing, Tammy and Geronimo dos Santos disappear. Her loser boyfriend is found tortured and shot in the heart, there is blood on the floor that is probably hers, but there is no trace of her body, and the case goes cold. Until two years later, when an anonymous client employs a disreputable shamus to investigate the loser's murder. I call that a mindfuck."

I had to agree. "And the only person with any credible motive for killing her is Peter, her husband. But if it was him, what the hell is with this whole circus?"

We were quiet for a bit. Then she asked me, "Do you like him for it?"

"Peter?"

She nodded.

"So far, it's the only thing that makes sense. The only theory that holds water, as of right now, is that dos Santos was planning to use Tammy in a scam. She was only meant to get close to Duffy, but as everybody keeps telling us, she was so radiant and luminous it went too far, too fast, and they were both swept off their feet." I shrugged, thinking it through, gazing at the sidewalk but seeing the scenes playing themselves out in my mind's eye. "She still has feelings for Steve, and before committing to Duffy, she decides to pay a flying visit to her old lover to see if he will reconsider."

The waitress came out with two steaming bowls of mussels and fresh cream. She set them down, and when she'd gone, I continued.

"Thing is, Peter has had a bellyful. He follows her to New

York, finds them together, and kills them. Like you said before, in all this miasma of people and weird situations, there is only one motive. The oldest motive on Earth."

We ate, not so much in silence, as in slurping. When I had finished off my bowl, I sat licking my fingers. "I don't see we have anything left to do here in San Francisco."

She sat back and sipped her beer. "We know who she is, we know why she went to New York, at least in general terms, and we have a possible suspect. What are we going to do about him?"

"Hank has to get back to us."

"On whether Peter has priors and whether he owns a gun."

I nodded. "Mm-hm. If we get a positive on those two, then we can ask for a court order to see if he used a credit card to buy a ticket to New York in June 2015."

"Makes sense. At least that's solid ground."

I smiled. "Let me complicate things a little, then. Here's a thought. How do you like Geronimo dos Santos for Baxter's client?"

She thought about it while the waitress took our plates away and delivered two peppered steaks. I asked for two more beers. Dehan leaned forward and picked up her knife. She pointed it at me like a fencing foil.

"It's got to be somebody, right?" I made a "that's logical" face and cut into my steak. "Somebody who is looking for Tammy. I'm stating the obvious, but in this case, you kind of have to."

"I agree."

"So we know it's not Duffy, because he didn't know she was in New York. And we know it wasn't Peter because . . . why?"

I spoke with my mouth full. "Because if he killed her, why would he start an investigation? And if he didn't—he's moved on, he wants to get married—why would he look for her?"

"Yeah." She nodded. "So who does that leave?"

I raised my eyebrows at her. "Geronimo dos Santos. So where does that lead us?"

She stuck a forkful of steak into her mouth and spoke around it. "If he is looking for her, he either wants her, or he wants some-thing she has."

"What's the bet that Duffy lied? What's the bet she took something from him?"

"Something Geronimo sent her to get in the first place."

"Mm-hm. That's my thinking."

She screwed up her face. "It doesn't make a lot of sense. We are back to what Duffy himself said. Why steal something you already own?"

I gave a small shrug. "Because what she really wanted was Stephen Springfellow. And she thought if she could take him some prize, something really valuable, he might take her back."

"That's pathetic."

"I don't know if Stanford has done a study on it yet—it might be considered politically incorrect—but you and I both know that there is a sad tendency among women to throw their lives away on losers. Nothing, it seems, is more attractive to a woman than a deadbeat, parasitical layabout. And if he beats her up occasionally, so much the better."

She stared at me for a bit. "That's pretty harsh."

"Am I wrong?"

She shook her head. "No. You're probably right."

"So we should do some background research on dos Santos too, when we get back, and run the DNA on the brush to match it with Tamara's."

We ordered coffee and I called the captain to let him know we would be catching the next flight back. He told me if he was in my shoes, he'd invent reasons for staying. They had topped 95 degrees Fahrenheit, and the air-conditioning was still not fixed.

We walked back to where I had left the car, at Alta Plaza Park, and drove back sedately toward the Hillsdale Inn. Neither of us seemed in an awful hurry to book the tickets back.

In the end, Dehan made the reservations when we got back to the hotel. The flight was at six p.m., which meant we'd be getting in just before midnight. While she was down at reception printing the boarding passes, I phoned Hank to thank him for his help.

"I was just about to call you, actually, Stone. I got an answer to your queries. Peter Gunthersen has owned a Colt .38 revolver for the last five years. He's a member of the gun club. As to priors, there were a couple of domestic incidents, and he's been in a couple of brawls, but nothing serious."

I thanked him and hung up.

Nothing serious, I thought, except maybe a double homicide.

ELEVEN

THE NEXT COUPLE OF DAYS WERE HOT, HUMID, AND slow. The air-con was still not fixed. We dropped the hairbrush off at the lab and asked Frank nicely if he would prioritize it. He said he would, along with the fifteen other priorities he had going. We talked to the captain and laid out the case so far for him. He had a mildly incredulous squint on his face throughout most of it. In the end, he agreed to seek a court order to view Peter Gunthersen's credit card and bank account details for the months of May and June 2015. He would also talk to the San Mateo PD about getting a warrant to run a ballistics test on Peter's .38.

Then all we could do was wait. Wait, perspire, and look for Geronimo dos Santos. But he was not easy to find.

A couple of days rolled by. I tried the Jesuits, but they were politely vague and gently unhelpful, suggesting I try various different departments and archives, usually in writing, and managing to convey a feeling that my pursuit was not a very hopeful one.

Dehan searched on Google and found a Brazilian mixed martial arts fighter who didn't look much like a Jesuit collector of rare tomes.

I called Bernie at the bureau.

"Hey, Stone, long time. You only call me when you need something. You're not the only man in my life, you know?"

"Honey, don't talk like that. You know it makes me sad."

He gave a fat laugh and rounded it off with, "What do you want, Stone?"

"A Jesuit priest, a collector of rare books, probably Portuguese or Spanish, name of dos Santos, Geronimo. Ring any bells?"

He made a long "pffff" sound. "Off the top of my head, ol' buddy, not the slightest chime. I can have a snoop around, get back to you if any flags pop up."

"Appreciate it, Bernie."

"You owe me."

"I know. I'll buy you something nice. Frilly."

He gave another fat laugh, and I hung up. Dehan was watching me.

"You really do need a woman in your life."

"I already have a woman in my life. You think I need another one?"

My phone rang. I looked at the screen. It was Frank. I put him on speaker.

"What have you got, Frank?"

"Okay, the hairbrush."

"Good, what?"

"Not a match."

I stared at Dehan.

"The blood on the carpet and the hair on the brush are *not* from the same person." He waited. I was silent, trying to process the implications. He went on. "I don't know why the blood from the floor was not processed back in 2015, but it wasn't. It is clearly not Springfellow's. We ran it through CODIS and we got a hit."

"You did? Who?"

"Ernesto Sanchez, a member of the Sureños gang." Dehan and I were still staring at each other. I heard Frank say, "Stone? You still there?"

"Yeah. Yeah, thanks, Frank. That's . . ."

"Clearly not what you expected."

"You could say that."

"Sorry!"

He hung up.

"Mindfuck is right, Dehan."

She was already on the computer, checking the database. "I remember Ernesto Sanchez. He was a real asshole. He lived a couple of streets from me. He had an older brother, Alfonso, another asshole. They used to hang out and be assholes together. If I remember rightly . . ." She stopped talking and stared at the screen. "Yeah, Alfonso is in jail, Attica, upstate. He's halfway through a two-year sentence."

"What about Ernesto?"

She shook her head. "He's been off the radar for a while." She got up and went and stuck her head out the door. She looked around a bit and suddenly bellowed, "Hey, Chavez! Come here!"

She came back to the desk, and after a moment a uniformed cop walked into the detectives' room. He looked as though he was trying not to look pissed.

"Yes, Detective."

"You patrol Garrison Avenue, Bryant Hill Garden, Seneca . . ." She made an "and so on" gesture with her hand. "Right?"

He nodded. "Sure."

"You know the Sanchez boys, Alfonso and Ernesto?"

He frowned. "Yeah. Alfonso's inside."

I said, "What about Ernesto? You seen him around?"

He pulled a face. "Now you mention it . . . I ain't seen him for a while."

"How long, would you say?"

Chavez looked embarrassed. "I'm sorry, Detectives, I couldn't say."

Dehan said, "More than a year?"

He nodded. "I'd say so."

"More than two?"

He danced his head from side to side. "Maybe a couple of years."

I reached for my phone. "Thanks, Chavez. That's great."

He left, looking uncertain.

"Dehan, we want an APB on Ernesto Sanchez. I want to know if he is dead or alive. If he's alive, I want to talk to him."

"I'm on it!"

"Meantime, I am going to call Attica."

She grinned. "Road trip!"

I arranged a meeting with Alfonso Sanchez for the following day at twelve noon, which meant setting out at six or six thirty a.m. I hung up and looked at my watch. It was only five, but I was beat. Dehan stretched and cracked her vertebrae over the back of her chair, then went to stand in front of the fan with her arms held out.

I said, "We've got an early start. Up at five. You want to stay over?"

She yawned and gave me the thumbs-up.

We stopped at Kmart on the way and bought some groceries. Dehan led the way, talking over her shoulder as I followed. "I thought maybe spaghetti? It's easy, but it's filling. What do you think? Or maybe baked potatoes, but it takes at least an hour. I think spaghetti. You got any preference?"

I smiled but didn't bother answering because she'd already put the ingredients in the basket and was walking toward the wine section.

"I don't normally drink wine midweek, Stone, but spaghetti without wine? It's like oysters without champagne, burger without beer. It's not right, is it?"

"No."

"They say the man should choose the wine. I don't see why. Women can't choose wine? Plus, you're just standing there like Friday on Monday. I like this one."

She chose a wine.

"Like Friday on Monday?"

"My dad used to say it. What does Friday do on Monday?"

"Not a lot."

"Exactly. I also need a toothbrush and shampoo." She grinned. "Don't worry. I won't leave them in your bathroom." I followed her back toward the checkout. "Most men, you start leaving your toothbrush and your shampoo at their house, they freak out."

WHEN WE GOT to my house, she went to the kitchen and started unpacking. I said, "You want a drink?"

"What you got there?"

"Beer, whiskey, martini, gin . . ."

She opened the fridge. "I found the beer."

She cracked it and drank from the bottle. I poured myself a whiskey. She had started chopping onions on a wooden board. I wandered into the kitchen and leaned against the fridge, watching her.

"So, Stone, for real. What's the deal with you and women?"

I was surprised and let my face show it, but she was staring at the onions she was chopping and didn't see me. After a moment, I shrugged.

"There is no deal . . ."

"That's kind of my point."

"It's like I told you before. I was married. It didn't work out. And as you know yourself, this job kind of gets in the way."

She made a face. "For me it wasn't the job. I just never met a guy who wasn't a jerk."

I smiled. "Maybe it's the same for me. I never met a woman who wasn't a jerk."

She threw the onions into the olive oil, followed by garlic and red peppers, then added some fresh thyme. It smelled good.

"But," she said and paused a moment, grinding black pepper into the meat, "don't you ever miss *having* somebody? Like, you know, even just a companion. Hell! The sex! Don't you miss the sex?"

"This is very personal, Dehan."

"Do you mind?"

I shook my head. "No. No, I don't mind." I thought about it. "I guess the answer is, if I stop and think about it, yes, of course I do. But—" I laughed. "Thankfully I have a job that doesn't give me much time to think about it."

She nodded but didn't say anything. She stirred the onions, then dropped in the meat and started breaking it up with the wooden spatula. I watched her a moment, then said, "Why do you ask, Carmen?"

She danced her head around a bit.

"We work together. We see into other people's lives and tragedies probably more intimately than anybody else in *their* lives." She paused, shrugged, and made a face. "You know a lot about me. More than anybody else alive, or dead! But I don't know a lot about you."

I stared into my whiskey. "Maybe there isn't much to know."

"Open the tins of tomatoes for me, would you? And just grind some black pepper into them."

I smiled and did as she asked. As I was grinding the pepper, she said, "You do know, right, if you ever need to talk . . ."

I handed her the tomatoes, and as she poured them over the meat, I said, "I'm not gay."

She laughed. It was a funny, infectious laugh that made me laugh too. She put her hand on my arm. "I know."

We stared at each other a moment, smiling.

I said, "I'll set the table."

TWELVE

We were up at five, and Dehan performed her ritual of frying bacon and eggs and making coffee. To me, breakfast is a slice of toasted rye and a large espresso, but I was beginning to enjoy the ritual as much as she obviously did, so I wasn't about to complain.

By six, we were on the road, moving through a dark city that was yawning and stretching and fumbling its way to the bathroom. We took the Cross Bronx Expressway over the Alexander Hamilton and the George Washington, and then we followed the I-80 through endless suburbs, heading west and north. We didn't say a word to each other until we had left Totowa behind us and we were driving among countryside and thick woodlands touched by the early-morning sun.

Then I eased back in my seat and said, "We need to address the elephant in the room."

She turned to look at me. "What?"

"It looks as though Baxter sent us on a wild goose chase. We have absolutely no reason to believe that Tamara Gunthersen had anything to do with Stephen's murder. Or am I wrong?"

She grunted. After a bit, she said, "Her husband still has a Colt .38. She still probably came here to see Stephen."

I glanced at her. "Did she shoot Ernesto Sanchez?" She shrugged. "This walking ray of divine sunshine shot a Sureño?"

Mindfuck was right.

We didn't discuss it again until we reached Attica. We left the car in the parking lot, showed our badges at the gate, and a warden showed us across the yard into one of the wings. From there, we were taken to a secure interview room with concrete walls and no windows. A fluorescent strip on the ceiling gave a dead, stark light over a table and three chairs.

After five minutes, steel doors clanged and echoed, and Alfonso Sanchez was led in. He was seated opposite us and handcuffed to the table. He was in his thirties, but he looked older. He had a Fu Manchu moustache and a tattooed face. He wasn't somebody you'd want your daughter to date.

"We've been looking for your brother, Ernesto."

He smiled. The question amused him. "You bin lookin' for Ernesto? You found him?"

"He went off the radar two years ago."

The smile faded and he shrugged. "What can I tell you, cop? I don't know nothin'." He gestured around him. "I'm inside. What do I know?"

Dehan said, "You could tell us if he's dead. Is he dead, or was he just injured?"

He hissed through his teeth and looked away.

She pressed him. "Come on, Alfonso. I know you. I saw you every fuckin' day when we were growing up. You went everywhere together. You did everything together. You want me to believe you weren't there when he got shot?"

He was looking mad and scared at the same time. He didn't know what we knew, and he was seeing his sentence shifting from two years to twenty for the murder of Stephen Springfellow.

I leaned across the table and spoke softly. "Did you and Ernesto murder Steve?"

"No! Uh-uh!" He was shaking his head.

I ignored him and went on. "Because right now, Ernesto's

blood and an eyewitness put you both at the scene of the murder."

He was still shaking his head. "Uh-uh, no way. I was there, and so was my bro, but I did not kill that motherfucker."

"But you beat him up."

"Yeah, we beat him. But we did not kill him. Shit! He weren't through talking to him . . ."

He knew he'd said too much, sighed, and shut his mouth.

Dehan gave a small laugh. "Okay, help me out here, Alfonso, because to be honest, things are not looking good for you right now. See, here's my problem. There is you, there is Ernesto, and there is Steve. Steve is tied to the chair, and you both are beating him . . ."

Alfonso was shaking his head.

Dehan ignored him. "Then what happens, Steve suddenly slips his bonds, shoots your brother, then shoots himself, and just before he dies, he ties himself up again? Come on, level with us, or you are going down for the double homicide of Steve *and* your brother."

He sighed. "*Hija de puta* . . ."

I growled, "Watch your tongue."

"We were not the only ones there." He looked real scared for a moment and leaned forward. "You gotta understand, this had *nothing* to do with the Sureños. This was just me an' Ernesto, doin' a private job."

Dehan snapped, "What kind of private job?"

"I'm comin' to that. But you got to understand, this is nothin' to do with the gang. Okay?"

I nodded. "I understand."

"It was Danny Schultz. He come to me and Ernesto in Pepe's Place. We knew him from when we were kids. He's a fuckin' loser. Always wheelin' and dealin' and always makin' a fuckin' loss." He laughed and I saw he had three teeth missing. "But he comes to me an' Ernesto an' he says he has a job. His employer—he call him his 'employer'—wants him to beat up some guy and find some chick. He says the pay is real good. Danny is no good for that kind of job." He turned to Dehan like they were old pals. "You know Danny, right? Skinny little fuck. So his employer tells him to go find some real pros. So he come to us."

Dehan's voice could have corroded stainless steel. "Yeah, you're real professionals. So the guy you had to beat up was Steve?"

"Yeah, Danny said this guy knew where the chick was."

"So what happened?"

He shrugged and pulled a face. He looked confused. "The whole thing was crazy. We get to the apartment and Danny knocks on the door, like he is going to visit his fockin' family. The guy opens the door and we go in. Danny is pushin' him. But the fuckin' chick is *there* in the apartment. So what the fuck? Now what?"

I stopped him. "Is this the girl?"

I showed him a photograph of Tammy.

He nodded. "Yeah, that's her. Cute chick."

Dehan said, "So what happened next?"

"Danny starts going crazy, screaming at both of them to tell where it is."

I stopped him again. "Where what is?"

He shook his head. "I dunno, man. He's just screaming, 'Where the fuck is it? Tell me where the fuck it is!' But they just keep sayin' they don't know what he's talkin' about. So Danny tells me and Ernesto to tie Steve to the chair. Now Steve is getting scared, right? So he changes his tune. Now he's sayin' *he* don't know where it is, but *she* does."

"Hang on." It was Dehan. "Did Danny tell you at any point who his employer was?"

Alfonso shook his head. "No, man, that was like, secret. But he made it sound like this guy had plenny money. That was not a consideration. An' this chick, she had something that he wanted real bad. So I'm thinking now we gonna have to beat up on the girl. But Danny has a different idea. He is gonna be smart. She is like crying and begging for them not to hurt Steve. She even gets down on her knees, and she is sayin' over and over, 'Please don't hurt him, please don't hurt him.' So Danny tells her he is going to beat Steve to death if she don't tell him where it is. All she does is cry. So Danny gives Steve a backhander . . ." He started laughing with real mirth. "The motherfucker almost breaks his fockin' hand. You could see the fockin' tears in his eyes, man. So he says to me and Ernesto to beat Steve to death, and don't stop until she talks."

Dehan shook her head. "But you didn't."

"No, man. We give him a good beating. Danny is standing by the door, smoking. Me and Ernesto is takin' it in turns, and Steve is in a bad way. She is on the floor, hysterical, cryin' and beggin', 'Please don't hurt him! Please don't hurt him!'" He turned to look at me with genuine bewilderment. "But who gets chicks, right? Suddenly, she's screaming, 'All right! All right!' like this, 'All right, I take you to it! Just stop hurting him!' And she goes to a chest of drawers, like she's gonna get some keys or some shit. And, I am swearing to you, man, she takes out a .38 from the drawer an' she plugs a hole right in Steve's chest. Right there! Like that, *pom!* Then she shoots Ernesto. Then she turns the gun on Danny, but he is out of there like fockin' shit, man."

Dehan narrowed her eyes. "She didn't shoot you . . ."

He shook his head slowly. "No, man, I bent down to help Ernesto and get him out of there. He's hurt bad. I look at her. She looks at me. Then she's gone. I don't know if she went after Danny or what she did. I just know I didn't die that night *porque Dios no lo quiso.*" He looked at me. "God didn't want it."

I drummed the table with my fingers. "Yeah, no doubt he's saving you for a sunbeam."

Dehan stared at me for a moment, then looked back at Alfonso. "You are telling me that after begging for him not to be hurt, she pulled a gun on you and shot *him* before she shot

Ernesto? She didn't shoot Ernesto, you, and Danny. She shot Steve."

He shrugged. "That's the way it happened, man. If I was going to lie to you, I would tell you something more convincing. She pulled the gun from the drawer, I'm thinkin', 'Fuck, I am going to die,' but then she points that thing at Steve and shoots him through the heart."

I sighed. "What happened to Ernesto?"

"The bullet was lodged in his chest. It come in through the side, tore up his lungs. He died. We put him in a sack and buried him in the river."

We were quiet for a bit. Eventually, I asked him, "Where can we find Danny Schultz?"

"He used to hang out at Pepe's Place, on Longwood, by the railway bridge."

"Okay." I stood.

"Hey, Stone, I know you ain't gonna believe me. But losin' my bro like that . . ." He jerked his head at Dehan. "She'll tell you. Me and him, we was close, man, real close. Losin' him and then having my life spared like that . . . when I get out of here, I am goin' straight. I didn't kill Steve. I done bad things and I gotta atone for them, and I will. But I did not kill Steve."

When we got to the door, he called out, "An' I cooperated with you! Right?"

I looked back at him and nodded.

Down in the parking lot, Dehan leaned her ass against the car and crossed her arms. In the glaring heat, against the burgundy of the Jag, her hair looked very black.

"Is it me? Am I going crazy? Or is it the world? You know, maybe it's normal. Maybe it's normal for a sweet girl that everybody describes as luminous to pull out a .38 and blow away the man she's supposed to love. Maybe I'm the crazy one."

I opened the door and climbed in. As she got in next to me, I said, "You're not crazy, Dehan. We've been chasing ghosts and shadows."

"You're not kidding! The one motive we had, the one solid thing we had to hold on to, just got flushed down the can!"

I fired up the engine and looked at my double reflection in her shades. "But it never was the motive."

THIRTEEN

It was six p.m. and as hot as midday by the time we cruised down Longwood Avenue in the Bronx and pulled up in front of Pepe's Place. It was shady and quiet, empty apart from a couple of old guys sitting in the corner drinking beer and minding their own business. The place was seedy, but clean, and there were posters of Jimi Hendrix and Janis Joplin on the walls.

Pepe was one of those rarest of men who walked his own path in life and managed to retain the respect of everybody who knew him. The Sureños drank in his bar, but they left him alone, and the cops knew he was clean and let him be. Even Mick, back in the day, steered clear of him.

He was a big Mexican with an ugly scar on his face. Rumor was he had done some ugly things back home and had to leave. But nobody was in a hurry to find out if it was true or not. Pepe was not a man you questioned. As we stepped through the door, he was polishing glasses. He looked at Dehan and recognized her.

"*Hola*, Carmen." He gave me the once-over. "John, you want a drink or you want to ask me questions?"

I climbed on a stool, and Dehan leaned on the bar next to me. I said, "How about both? Let's have a couple of beers."

He pulled two draughts, and while he was at it, Dehan asked him, "Danny Schultz around?"

He glanced at her and finished pouring before he answered. He gave us our drinks and wiped the bar dry around the pump.

"Danny's dead."

I frowned. "Since when?"

He made a face that said he was thinking. "Eighteen months?"

"What happened?"

He gave a snort and leaned against the till. "You're cops. You know how it is. With guys like Danny, if there ain't some direct eyewitness, or some proof they can find right there and then, they shelve the case and leave it. Forty percent of cases don't get solved for the same reason. The cops in hoods like this, they don't even try. I'm sorry, I don't wanna be offensive, and I can kinda understand it, you know? People don't make it easy. Nobody talks, nobody saw nothin', nobody heard nothin'." He shrugged. "But if you want my opinion, he was screwing the wrong chick."

Dehan glanced at me, then back at Pepe. "Danny *Schultz*? Danny never screwed anything but the IRS in his whole life."

Pepe smiled and shrugged. "He got lucky. I saw it with my own eyes. If I hadna seen it, I wouldn't believe it either. Danny Schultz. He was sitting right there, where you're sitting now, complaining about taxes or the weather or whatever. I never listened to the *pendejo*. Then this chick comes in. Real sweet, real class, you know what I'm saying? Nicely dressed. Not a *puta* like these chicks you see 'round here. Nice. You could take her anywhere and feel proud, right?"

Dehan looked impatient. She was nodding. "So what happened?"

"She sits next to Danny and orders a martini." He laughed. "I don't think I ever served a martini before. She had to tell me how to prepare it. So Danny—" He looked at Dehan. "You know Danny, he knows everything, right? He starts explaining about the different martinis and how to make them, how much gin, how much vermouth, one olive, two olive, and he's sayin' something about James Bond drinks a Bradford martini, shaken, not stirred. Some shit. Anyway, I'm going to tell him to leave the lady in peace, when I see she's liking it. She's laughing like she thinks he's cute. 'Who would have told me,' she says, 'I was gonna come into a bar in the Bronx and meet a guy who's an expert on cocktails?'"

I reached in my pocket and pulled out the picture of Tamara Gunthersen. "This the woman?"

He stared at it a moment, then shook his head. "Nah. This chick had black hair cut short and green eyes. That's the girl next door, cute, nice. But this was a sophisticated woman, smart. She had class, you understand me? She sounded like Deep South, Louisiana, Alabama, something like that. With a real drawl, you know?"

"So what makes you think he saw her again?"

He looked at me with wide eyes and spread his hands. "They leave together!"

Dehan was incredulous and laughed. "They *left* together?"

"*Sí, hombre!* She's tellin' him about her car. Is a classic Mustang, he should see it. Also she is a little scared in this neighborhood alone. And she ask him why he don't go with her. So they go out together. An' that is the last time I ever see Danny Schultz. They found his body next morning." He gestured with his hand. For a moment he looked mad, like it was all wrong and that shouldn't have happened to Danny. "Twenty meters from here! In the yard next door. Shot through the heart."

Dehan was shaking her head. "Son of a gun . . ."

Pepe looked at me for a long moment. "You know, it don't make a lot of sense."

I nodded. "I agree, Pepe. It doesn't. Whichever way you look at it, it doesn't make sense."

"But the cops weren't interested, John. Is just Danny. Who's gonna miss Danny? So he got shot; he probably deserved it. You know what Chavez says to me? He probably tried to rape her. How can you write off a guy's life because of what he probably would of done?"

"You can't." I threw some coins on the counter. "Thanks, Pepe. Take it easy."

"Yeah, you too, John, Carmen."

In the car, Dehan said, "I am not even going to try."

I nodded as I fired up the engine. "I agree. I need a shower and a good sleep. We'll come at it fresh in the morning."

"Who the fuck is this woman now? Every time a door opens, it doesn't lead us closer to an answer; it lets in another character to make the damn case even more confusing!"

"We'll dig out Danny's case. It must be in the cold cases file. We'll get the lab to compare the two slugs."

"Steve and Danny?"

I nodded. "We need to get to Geronimo."

"And Tammy."

I looked at her. She was right.

I dropped her at her apartment, and she hesitated a moment before getting out. She smiled suddenly. "It's been fun. We should do it again sometime."

I laughed out loud. "You're some kind of crazy, Dehan."

The smile faded a little. "I mean what I said. If you ever need to talk . . ."

I punched her gently on the shoulder. "Okay, partner. Good to know."

As I drove back toward Morris Park and Haight Avenue, I thought about Geronimo dos Santos and Tamara Gunthersen. They were the linchpins in the case. Everything hung on those two individuals. They were the dual keys to understanding the case.

And we knew next to nothing about dos Santos, but we had a superabundance of information about Tamara. Yet as we had discovered this evening, all that information was as good as useless, because the bottom line was, we still knew nothing about *her*. All the information we had was smoke.

Was she a ruthless sociopath? Or did she have good reason to kill Steve? Was it love that took her running back to him? Or was it some other, darker reason? Was she a victim, or was she a predator, preying on the people around her?

I thought of her house, her books, her scrapbook, her photograph. There was nothing there. In fact, it was the absence of any personality that was most striking about the house. I remembered Iago in Othello: "I am not what I am . . ."

And Geronimo, about whom we knew—what, exactly? That he was supposedly a Jesuit, that he was supposedly a collector of rare books, that he might be Portuguese or Spanish. That nobody that we knew, aside from Duffy, had ever laid eyes on him.

Which of the two was the most anonymous? Which the most deeply cloaked in shadows? What did they want? What was their motivation? What was their purpose? Were they working together, or were they enemies?

And then, who was this Southern belle, with the black hair and the green eyes, who had hunted down Danny Schultz and killed him for no apparent reason? Was she working for Geronimo dos Santos?

I pulled in outside my front door and sat drumming my fingers on the wheel. There was only one person I could think of who could answer those questions for me.

Baxter.

It was time to pay Baxter another visit. I was going to shake his tree and see which way he jumped.

FOURTEEN

I had a late breakfast of toast and coffee and called Frank at nine to ask him to make the ballistics comparison between the slug that killed Steve and the slug that killed Danny Schultz. Then I picked Dehan up outside her apartment.

"You got plans for this morning?" she said, as she slammed the door.

"Yeah, I talked to Frank about the ballistics comparison. Now I want to go and shake Baxter's cage. Why?"

"I was going to say, we need to go shake Baxter's cage."

I smiled and pulled away. "After we talk to him, I want you to get a cab back to the precinct and get a court order to check Peter Gunthersen's accounts."

She looked surprised. "What are you going to do?"

"I'm going to stay with Baxter. I want to see where he goes after we scare him, or if anybody visits him."

He was already in the office when we arrived, and looked surprised when we walked in.

"Detectives!" He smiled like a man who isn't amused. "I wish you'd called. I am just on my way out."

I smiled back with the same feeling and sat at his desk. "No, Baxter, you're not. We are going to talk."

He stood.

Dehan pulled up a chair and sat beside me. She looked up at him and said, "Sit."

He sat.

I said, "Tell me about Geronimo dos Santos."

All the blood drained from his face. He made like a goldfish for a moment, then shook his head in an "I have no idea who that is" fashion.

I said, "Are you about to lie to me, Baxter? I would think carefully before you do that. Because if I know that dos Santos is your client, and he is involved in a homicide and you lie to me, that's your license gone right there. Is it worth it?"

He swallowed. "Homicide?" He glanced at Dehan. "My client is interested in the case. That isn't the same as being involved . . ."

"How about Ernesto Sanchez's murder? How about Danny Schultz's murder?" I studied his face a moment. He looked scared. "Do you know what you are getting yourself into, Baxter?"

"I don't know anything about Ernesto Sanchez or Danny Schultz . . ."

Dehan snorted. "But Geronimo dos Santos sure does. You led us on a pretty wild goose chase, Baxter, but we unearthed a few things, and let me tell you, pal, you are running with the wolves on this one."

I nodded my agreement. "People who do odd jobs for dos Santos seem to wind up dead shortly after. Usually shot with a .38. Does that sound familiar?"

He was thinking, fast, but not clearly. He said, "Danny Schultz . . ."

He knew who he was. Dehan cut in, "He was shot through the heart. Just like Steve. Do you know who shot them?"

Before he could think about it, I said, "Let me make it easy for you, Baxter. You don't need to tell me whether Geronimo is your client; I already know he is. All you need to do is tell me about him. Who is he? Where is he? What is his deal? What's his game? Do that for me and I will let you keep your license."

"Jesus, Stone!"

"What's it going to be, Baxter?"

"I don't know that much, and that's the truth! Before you start threatening me again, the fact is I don't know much about him at all. He plays his cards real close to his chest. He's a weird fucking guy, I can tell you that much."

"Where is he from?"

He shrugged. "The name is Brazilian, but he talks a lot about Spain. About a castle near Santiago de Compostela, Soto Mayor or something like that. So maybe he's Spanish. I don't know. It belongs to the church, and he was a custodian of the library there."

"Where is he now?"

"All I can tell you is that he is in New York. Where, I have no idea."

"How do you contact him?"

"I don't. He contacts me."

Dehan cut in, "How often?"

He hesitated. "Once every day. Before you ask, I don't know what time. It's randomized."

I thought for a moment. "Would he agree to meet me?"

Baxter laughed. "No way. The minute I tell him you know about him, he will vanish."

"Don't tell him."

"I don't plan to."

"Will you give me permission to tap your phone?"

His jaw sagged. "No. I'll tell you what, Stone, I'll give you my license, you wipe your ass on it and then flush it down the can. What do you think it will do for my business if it gets out I let the fucking cops tap my phone?"

"Okay!" It was Dehan. "Keep your pantyhose on, Baxter. We need to talk to this guy. He's involved in a triple homicide. We could use your help."

He pulled a face. "Aw, you're breaking my heart, Detectives.

So go investigate! I'm not here to wet-nurse you. I got a business to run."

"How about Tammy? You find out anything about her?"

"No. How about you?"

"Nothing you don't know already."

"Jeez, and me just a one-man operation. Go figure."

"Okay, Baxter. Have it your way." I stood. "But be careful. If I am reading him right, and I am, dos Santos is a dangerous man. People around him and Tammy Gunthersen wind up dead."

He watched us leave. He looked scared.

Downstairs, it was already getting hot again. We got in the car, and I put the air-con on. I drove Dehan to the end of the road, and she jumped out to get a cab back to the 43rd. Meanwhile, I drove around the block, parked forty yards down the road, and waited. I waited for half an hour. At ten o'clock he came down, crossed the road, and climbed into his car, a cream Toyota. He headed south on Melrose. I let him get away a bit, then did a U-turn and followed at a distance. He joined Third Avenue and continued south all the way down to where it meets Morris Avenue. At 138th Street, he turned right and crossed the Madison Avenue Bridge. Over the river, he turned into 5th Avenue, and I followed him down all along Central Park as far as East 68th, where he turned left, and left again into Madison Avenue. He crossed East 69th and parked on the left. I stopped short of the junction and pulled over.

I saw him get out of his car and lope across the road to push into a shop. It was on the same side as me, so I couldn't make out the name or the window display. I got out and dodged through the traffic so I was opposite, but still forty or fifty yards away. There was a hot dog stand on the corner. It was a little early, but I bought one anyway and stood behind the stand, where I was hidden from sight but had a good view of the shop.

It was an antiques shop. Henderson & Girt, Fine Antiques. It had a plate glass front, and I could see Baxter through the window. He was talking to a woman. After a minute or two, he took out his wallet and seemed to give her a card. After that, he left.

I stood for a long while trying to fit this new piece into the puzzle. I couldn't, so I crossed the road and entered the shop. The woman was still standing there, staring out at the street, as though lost in thought. She looked as though she was in her mid to late twenties, fair, with pale skin, and exquisitely dressed. I watched her a moment and thought she was probably one of the most beautiful women I had ever seen. She turned and looked at me. I smiled. She blinked and said, "I'm sorry. I was miles away."

She was English. She spoke what the English call cut-glass English. It was as beautiful as she was. I smiled. "I'm glad you came back. I'd hate to have missed you."

She liked the compliment but didn't respond to it. She moved toward me. "Was there anything in particular you were looking for, or were you just browsing?"

She had taken in my clothes and noted they were unremarkable, not Armani and not Savile Row. So she wasn't real interested. I thought I'd stimulate it a bit and said, "I'm moving into a new apartment down the road, and I was looking for a nice dining table."

Her pupils dilated and she allowed the pleasure to show on her face. "May I ask where the apartment is?"

"Only if you come to dinner when I get my table."

"I'd love to. Can my husband come?"

"No."

Her cheeks colored and she stepped away. "Were you looking for something elaborately elegant, rococo, or more restrained in the English style?"

I followed her. "I like the English style, but not too restrained."

"We have this rather lovely Queen Anne. The line of the legs is quite exquisite."

I stood close to her. "I have a weakness for exquisite English legs, and these are some of the nicest I have ever seen."

She studied my face a moment, trying to read me, wondering how to respond. "Are we still talking about furniture, Mr. . . . ."

"I never was, Miss . . ."

"*Mrs.* Girt."

I pointed back toward the door. She nodded. I smiled. "Henderson lost out."

"You're at risk of overplaying your hand."

"I'm always at risk of doing something. My name is John."

She narrowed her eyes. "Is that how you make your money? By taking risks?"

"Would that make a difference?"

"It might."

Her eyes traveled past me to the plate glass window. I turned to follow her gaze. There was a big man of about sixty with a large belly and a yellow waistcoat lumbering across the road.

"Your husband."

Our eyes met and we read each other loud and clear. Girt pushed in to the chime of a bell and walked past us toward the office in back. I said, "I'll give some thought to your English legs, if I may . . ."

"You may."

". . . and I'll get back to you."

She picked up a card from the counter where the till stood and scrawled something on the back. She handed it to me and said, "Please do."

I left the shop smiling, with a bounce in my step. I may even have whistled a little ditty. I looked at what she'd written on the back. It just said "Emma" and a phone number.

FIFTEEN

I didn't leave. I sat in my car and waited, as the sun grew higher and the heat got hotter. At twelve thirty, I took off my jacket and loped across the road to get another hot dog. Then, I sat for another half hour, sweating and watching the shop.

She came out just after one. She climbed into a dark blue Lexus and took off up Madison Avenue, headed north. I followed her back the way I had come, over the Madison Avenue Bridge and back up Third Avenue. As I had suspected, she was going to see Baxter.

Sure enough, at the junction with 149th, she turned up Melrose and parked outside his block. I kept about fifty yards back and pulled in to wait and see what happened. She climbed out, ran the three steps to his building, and disappeared inside. She was in there for half an hour. Then she came out, climbed into her car, and did a U-turn, and I followed her all the way back to Madison Avenue. There she got out and went back into her shop.

My phone rang. It was Dehan.

"Where are you?"

"I'm on Madison Avenue. Why?"

"Madison Avenue?" She paused a moment. "Okay, I think we need to take another look at Peter Gunthersen."

"Okay, I'm on my way."

By the time I got back to the precinct, it was gone two. I found Dehan at her desk eating a sandwich and drinking coffee.

"What you got?"

She pointed at her full mouth and said, "You foisht."

I shrugged. "I followed him to an antiques shop on Madison Avenue. He spoke to the owner's wife, gave her a card, and left. I went in, chatted to her about Queen Anne furniture, and she gave me *her* card. Then, at one o'clock, I followed her to his office. She stayed half an hour and left."

She swallowed. "That's it?"

"What more do you want?"

"Impressions, thoughts?"

I shook my head. "Nothing for now. What about you?"

She stuffed the last of her sandwich in her mouth and threw a half a dozen sheets of paper, all stapled together, across the desk at me. They were Peter Gunthersen's credit card readout for May and June 2015. Several items had been highlighted. They were a return rail ticket from San Francisco to New York, a hired car, and a room in a cheap hotel. All for the period June 12 to 15.

"Any word from ballistics?"

"I called. They haven't got to it yet."

"Whatever reason he was here, it was not to kill Steve Gunthersen."

She frowned and sipped her coffee. "Okay. Why?"

"What motive could Alfonso have for telling us that elaborate story about Tammy killing Steve and Ernesto? There are two possible scenarios. One, where Ernesto and Alfonso were not there, in which case, why did he say they were? What does he gain by putting himself at the scene of Steve's murder—especially with such an unlikely story? It also begs the question, how did he know the details of the murder scene?"

She was nodding. "No, we take it as read that he was there."

"Okay, so if he was there, what happened? Peter was already there when he and Ernesto arrived with Danny? It plays out like Alfonso said, except that Peter was there too, and it's Peter who pulls a gun and shoots Steve and Ernesto. That is marginally more credible than Alfonso's story, but we have to ask, why the hell did Alfonso lie? What does he gain by protecting Peter?" I spread my hands. "He stands a much better chance of being believed by placing Peter at the scene, than by making out it was Tammy. By lying, he actually runs the risk of incriminating himself."

"By making it look like he did it."

"Exactly."

"So what the hell was Peter doing in New York?"

"I think I know. Ballistics will confirm it."

She waited, but I didn't say any more, and after a moment she asked, "So, who's the dame?"

"Emma Girt."

"Emma Girt? You think she has something to do with the case?"

"Hard to tell at this stage. He went to see her after we rattled him. Gave her a card. Then at lunchtime, she went straight to see him and they spent half an hour together. Maybe she's a client. Maybe she's *the* client. I don't know."

She studied my face. "Is there something you are not telling me?"

I frowned and for some reason felt guilty, which made me feel a flash of irritation for a moment. "No, of course not."

She didn't say anything, but her face told me she didn't believe me. My phone rang and I answered it gratefully.

"John, it's Frank. Your rottweiler has been on my case this morning. She is lovely to look at, but man! What an attitude!" He paused, then sounded worried. "You got me on speaker?"

"I know. No, I haven't."

"Good. Anyway, I have a result for you on the ballistics. The two slugs are a match. Stephen Springfellow and Danny Schultz were killed with the same weapon."

"Well, whadd'ya know. That's good news. Thanks, Frank."

I hung up and sat staring at my desk.

When Dehan spoke, there was an edge to her voice. "You going to tell me what he said, or is this something else you're going to keep to yourself?"

"I am not keeping anything to myself, Carmen. That was Frank . . ."

"I know. I saw his name on the screen. What did he want? Or is it private?"

"No! It's not private. He had the ballistics results. They are a match. Stephen and Danny Schultz were killed with the same weapon."

She waited. I thought. The pieces were fitting together, but the way they were fitting together didn't make a lot of sense. Dehan spread her hands. She was beginning to look mad.

"So do the ballistics results confirm your theory or not?"

"Yes!"

"Goddamn it, Stone! What is with you? Do I have to get on my fucking knees and beg?"

I shook my head. "I'm sorry, I was thinking." I sighed. "The reason Peter came to New York was to deliver the gun."

"What?"

"He came to deliver the .38."

"How does that make any sense, Stone?"

"I don't know yet. But so far, how does any of it make any sense? For Peter to be our killer, we need to ignore too many unexplained threads."

"With all due respect, Stone, I think you are ignoring the obvious threads."

"You don't need to respect me, Dehan. Just respect the facts. The fact is Alfonso told us he was there at the killing. Peter wasn't. But the victims were killed with Peter's gun. The conclusion is inescapable. Somebody else used Peter's gun. So why did Peter come to New York exactly when he did, during those dates?" I shrugged, shook my head. "If Peter killed Stephen, then did he also dress up as a Southern belle, pick up Danny Schultz at Pepe's Place, and shoot him in the yard next door?"

She sighed loudly. She looked pissed. "You're saying he came all the way from Frisco to deliver his gun to Tammy, so she could kill the man she was crazy about . . . ? *Why?* Why would he do that? Why would *she* do that?"

"That's the million-dollar question."

Her face flushed. "And you're going to answer it by talking to an antiques dealer on Madison Avenue?"

I watched her a moment, aware that we had lost our rapport for some reason and not sure why, or how to get it back. The damn heat wasn't helping.

"I don't know. Maybe."

"You going to keep tailing her?"

"For now, yeah."

"You going to do it alone?"

I frowned. "No. But when I talk to her, for now, I'll do it alone."

"Right." She sighed again. She was beginning to look really mad. "Maybe I should go back to Frisco and talk to Peter. I could ask the local PD to bring him in for questioning." I nodded but didn't answer. She pointed at me with her pen. "You better be thinking with your brain, Stone, and not with your fucking dick. Because if you're not, I am going to hit you so hard your head is going to be spinning for a week! You're going to have corkscrew fucking neck syndrome."

I attempted a smile. She didn't respond.

"I hear you, Dehan."

"Don't fucking patronize me."

I sighed. "Okay, you're mad at me, and I am not sure why. Here is what we do. We have enough with his trip to New York and ballistics to request that he be taken in and transferred to New York for questioning. Whether he came to kill Stephen or to deliver the gun, we still need to talk to him as a material witness. Will that satisfy you?"

She nodded. "At least now it sounds like you're thinking with your brain. What's she like, anyway?"

I made a "you got this all wrong" face. "You are letting your imagination run away with you, Dehan."

"Hey! It makes no odds to me, Stone. It would do you good to get laid. I just don't want this dame fogging your thinking."

"*Fogging my thinking?* I spoke to her for five minutes."

"It takes a person six seconds to decide they want to get in another person's pants. I read that somewhere."

"Well, I don't want to get in her pants. I just want to know why Baxter is interested in her, and I will find that out tomorrow. End of story. Are we cool?"

She curled her lip and grunted. That was the best I was going to get.

"Come on, let's go talk to the captain."

SIXTEEN

That afternoon, we took care of the paperwork and the formalities and made the arrangements for Peter Gunthersen to be taken into custody as a material witness and transferred to the 43rd Precinct. San Mateo PD told us they would be in touch as soon as they had made the arrangements.

In the evening, I dropped Dehan at her apartment and told her I wouldn't pick her up in the morning. I was going to go straight to Madison Avenue. She said, "Sure," slammed the door, and was gone.

Next morning, I got up late, breakfasted toast and coffee, showered, and slapped on my most expensive aftershave. Then, I selected my most expensive suit. It wasn't really expensive, but it was better than what I wore to work every day. At ten o'clock, I set off at a leisurely pace for Madison Avenue.

I parked across the road and strolled in at half past ten. She smiled and looked pleased to see me. "Mr. Stone . . ."

"John. Hello, Emma."

"Did you make up your mind about the table?"

I went and stood really close to her. She didn't step back. I said, "Did you?"

She gave a small laugh and looked at the buttons on my shirt. "What do you want, Mr. . . . John?"

I sighed and went to look at the Queen Anne table. It was exquisite. It probably cost more than my car. "I'm looking for something special."

"Can you be a little more precise?"

"Not really. I'll know it when I see it." I turned to face her. "But I am pretty sure that you are the person to find it for me."

She was thoughtful for a moment. "What gives you that idea?"

I shrugged. "Well, Emma, you're pretty special yourself." She smiled, but there was a certain caution in her eyes. "Also . . ." I ran my fingers over the high polish on the tabletop. I was going to take a risk, and I was only 90 percent sure of what I was doing. "I have searched high and low, far and wide . . ." I turned to look her in the eye so there would be no mistake. "I have been as far as San Francisco, searching . . . and something tells me I have finally found the right person."

She was shaken. She went pale, but she hid it well. "Who do you work for, John?"

I planted a smile on the left side of my face; that's where it looks most rueful. "You wouldn't believe me if I told you."

"Really? Then tell me so that I can think of you as a liar."

"I'm a cop."

She frowned. For a fraction of a second, I could see her reviewing everything I had said and done since the day before.

Then, I added, "But I work for myself."

She cooled noticeably. "Mr. Stone, I don't know what you think you are onto, or what you think you are doing, but you have obviously made a mistake."

I switched my smile to the other side of my face, which is where it looks ironic.

"Really? Now I'm the one who's thinking of you as a liar."

"Mr. Stone . . ."

"John."

"I really don't need to stand here and be insulted."

"You can sit if you like. Why don't you tell me about Baxter?"

Her face went rigid. "Who?"

"You heard me, Emma. Karl Baxter, private investigator. He was in here yesterday just before I came in. He gave you a card and left. You went to see him at lunchtime."

Her cheeks colored and her eyes were bright. "Have you been spying on me?"

"What if I have?"

"Why, I should . . . !"

"Call the cops? I am the cops, remember?" I pulled out my badge and showed it to her. As she stared at it, I said, "But I'm a bad cop."

"What do you want from me?"

"I told you, something special."

"Are you trying to blackmail me?"

I narrowed my eyes at her and considered her for a long while. Finally, I said, "You want to explain to me what it is exactly that I have on you that I could use for blackmail?"

"Stop playing games with me."

"You have no idea how much I know, Emma, do you?" I waited, and she just kept staring, with flushed cheeks and eyes bright with threatened tears. And I kept thinking I had never seen a woman quite so beautiful. "I know about Tammy." I studied her face for a reaction. "I know about Peter and Steve, and about Danny. And I know about Hugh. I know everything."

"You can't . . ."

"I can't what? I told you, I'm a cop. Digging up shit is what I do for a living."

"All right, you have my attention! So why don't you tell me once and for all what it is you *want*?"

I walked back to her and stood really close so we were touching. I felt her tremble and took hold of her arms, pressing her closer. "I want in. I want to be a part of it."

Her voice was a harsh whisper. "I don't know what you're talking about . . ."

I took out one of my cards and slipped it into the low-cut neckline of her dress. I heard her breath shudder and smiled at her.

"I can help you, baby. That schmuck of a husband of yours ain't going to cut it. You need me, and you know it. You knew it the minute I walked through that door."

She shook her head. "No . . ."

"Think about it. Call me tonight."

I walked out and crossed the road. As I climbed in my car, I could see her staring through the glass at me.

When I got back to the station, Dehan was at the desk writing up her notes on the case. She glanced at me as I sat down, and carried on writing.

"San Mateo PD called. They pulled Peter in last night. They'll be here by five."

"Good."

She continued writing. "You got something to report, or is it private?"

"No, it's not private, Dehan. Will you stop saying that already? I just don't know what it is."

She gave half a nod. She wrote in silence for a bit. After a while, she said, "Well, if you ever find out what it is, or decide you'd like to work with a partner, you let me know."

"Dehan, what is eating you?"

She threw down her pen hard enough to make it bounce. "What is eating me? *Seriously?* You open up a whole new angle on this investigation. You completely exclude me from it. And all you have to tell me is that you don't know 'what it is.' Well, from where I am sitting, it looks like it's enough to have you most of yesterday afternoon on a stakeout. And it's enough to have you all this morning doing whatever you've been doing in your best suit and your most expensive aftershave. But it's not enough for you to tell your partner about. It's enough for you"—she poked her finger at me—"to conduct your own private investigation, but it's not enough for you to keep me in the loop about it."

"I'm sorry, Dehan."

She spread her hands. "So, what is this angle on the investigation that is enough to keep you so busy, but is not enough for me to be kept informed about it?"

"You're right. I should have kept you in the loop. But it's hard to explain." She raised an eyebrow at me. I tried to ignore her and pressed on. "It's just a hunch. Well, it's a bit more than a hunch now."

"So, what is it?"

"I told you Baxter went to see this woman, then she went to see him."

"Uh-huh."

"So I went in to talk to her. She's young, attractive, and she's married to the owner of the antiques shop, who is almost three times her age and one of the best-known experts in antiques in New York."

"So?"

"Give me a break, Dehan, I'm explaining. So I went in this morning and made a play."

She raised her eyebrows. "You made a play? What does that mean?"

"It means I came on to her, but I played the bent cop, told her I knew what she was about. I knew about Peter, Tammy, Steve, and Ernesto, and also about Hugh. I didn't use any of their surnames, just their first names. She knew what I was talking about."

She frowned. "How do you know?"

I gave a small shrug. "She was cagey, but she didn't look at me as though I was crazy. She asked me if I was blackmailing her, and what I wanted."

"What did you tell her?"

I gave a small laugh. "It wasn't easy. Fact is, I don't know. I don't know what part she plays in this, but I am sure as hell she has some part to play. And so is Baxter. I gave her my card and told her to call me tonight."

She stared out the window at a street suffering from heat exhaustion. "You should have told me about this."

I spread my hands and shrugged. "Told you what? I had a hunch she had something to do with it. That was it."

She sighed.

I sighed too. "I think, I *feel*, she has some connection with Tamara. She even looks a bit like her. But I have no idea what that connection is. That's what I hope to find out tonight."

She stared at me. "Stone, look me in the eye and tell me you are not getting emotionally involved with this woman."

I looked at her like she was an idiot, held her eye, and said, "Stop worrying, Dehan. I am not getting emotionally involved with this woman. Satisfied?"

She watched me a moment, then said, "No. Let's get some lunch."

SEVENTEEN

PETER GUNTHERSEN WAS BROUGHT IN AT SIX P.M. WE
signed for him, and Sergeant Henderson took him to interview
room three, upstairs. Dehan and I gathered our notes and went
up to talk to him. He was perspiring and didn't look pleased to see
us. As we sat opposite him, he said, "Am I under arrest?"

I shook my head. "No, you're being held as a material witness.
But I can tell you, in light of recent developments in the case, that
it is in your best interest to cooperate fully with us."

"Do I need a lawyer?"

"No, but it's your right to have one if you want one. I am not
planning on charging you with anything, Peter. I just want to ask
you some questions."

He stared at Dehan a moment, then said, "Okay."

I scratched my chin, organizing my thoughts.

"You want to tell me again about your relationship with
Tamara, and when you last saw her?"

He closed his eyes, puffed out his cheeks, and blew.

"I just got so damn sick of her." He opened his eyes and stared
at me, as though he had given me some kind of cogent explanation. "She was—" He took a moment, looking around the room
to find words that could express his feelings. "Heavenly. You

know what I mean? She was like no woman I ever met, and she made me happy like no other woman. But when she changed, at first I couldn't handle it and I didn't want to let her go. So I refused to give her a divorce, like I told you."

Dehan said, "But . . . ?"

He sighed and shook his head and looked sad, really regretful. "In the end, she was so full of shit, I agreed. I met Tasha—I fell in love with a *real* woman, who was loyal and true and wasn't playing fucking games all the time—and I agreed to give Tammy a divorce. But she turns around now and says no."

"When was this?"

"About the time she disappeared. About the time she got that crazy gig she was going on about, that was going to change her life."

I glanced at Dehan to see if she was going to ask. She was watching me. I said, "So did she put any kind of condition on giving you your divorce?"

He nodded. "I guess you know she did. The condition was that I give her my revolver. I told her I would not, and I asked the crazy bitch what she wanted it for. She said she was in the Bronx in New York; it was a dangerous place to be alone, and she wanted protection."

Dehan frowned. "She said she was alone?"

"That's what she said. I asked her if she wasn't with Steve, and she said things weren't working out like she'd hoped. She was alone and scared and just needed the revolver for protection. She told me if I would just bring it to her, she would grant me the divorce and bring it back to me when she returned to San Francisco."

"So that's what you did."

"You know I did, or I wouldn't be here."

I said, "Where did you meet? Did you go to her place?"

"She had an apartment on . . ." He paused to think. "Intervale Avenue, opposite the church there. I gave her the gun and begged her not to do anything stupid. And that was it."

Dehan gave him a "not really" smile. "You booked your return for three days."

He gave a snort. "To be honest, I was hoping I could convince her to come back to San Francisco with me. I gave myself an extra day hoping we could meet and talk and maybe I could persuade her to stop being such a crazy bitch. But I never had a hope in hell. I spent most of my time in Central Park feeding the ducks. Then I went home. I've been waiting ever since for the divorce papers. Is she dead? Was she killed with my gun? Is that why I'm here?"

He had gone a pale gray color.

Dehan shook her head. "No, Peter, we are no longer convinced that Tammy is dead. We don't know what has happened to her. Does the name Danny Schultz mean anything to you?"

"No. Should it?"

"How about Ernesto Sanchez?"

He squinted at her like she was crazy. "No. Why?"

I leaned forward. "Peter, while you were in New York, did you at any time go and see Stephen Springfellow?"

He looked genuinely astonished. "Are you kidding me? Why would I want to go and see that son of a bitch?"

I pulled a face. "Maybe to shoot and kill him?"

"*What?*"

"Stephen's body was found two years back, while you were still in New York. He had been shot with your gun."

He went white and slumped back in his chair, shaking his head. "Oh, no, no! No, I did not! I would not! No, no way, man . . ."

Dehan cut across him. "Can you think of any reason why Tammy would want to kill Stephen?"

He did a double take. "What? *No!* Of course not!"

Dehan pressed on. "Would it surprise you to know that Tammy was also engaged to be married to Hugh Duffy?"

He gaped at her for a moment and then burst out laughing.

He stared from Dehan to me and then back again. "What? Are you trying to drive me crazy? Is this some new kind of interrogation technique? Make me lose my sense of reality?"

We both watched him without smiling.

He stopped laughing and became serious. "You mean it? Hugh Duffy? *The* Hugh Duffy . . . ?"

I nodded. "Yes. That was the gig."

He narrowed his eyes at me, like he was struggling to understand. "Who the hell was I married to, Detective Stone?"

I sucked my teeth and nodded. "That is what we would like to know, Peter. One last question . . ." I glanced at Dehan. "Unless . . . ?" She shook her head, so I went on. "There is a woman we are interested in talking to. She is best described as a Southern belle type. Alabama, Louisiana, strong accent. Black hair, probably cut short. Green eyes. A lot of class and elegance. Very attractive. Ring any bells?"

He frowned, staring at me like he thought I was setting a trap for him. After a moment, he said, "No. I don't know anybody like that."

I nodded. "We'll keep you overnight, Peter, but unless something comes up, I am pretty sure we can send you home tomorrow."

I called the sergeant, and she led him away down to the holding cells. Dehan stood and walked around the room, staring at the walls, like there were invisible pictures there only she could see. "You were right." She said it to the wall. "He was delivering the gun."

"It made sense. It was the most likely explanation."

She turned to face me. "So who are all these other women? And how do they tie in with Geronimo dos Santos? What has he got, some kind of female league of assassins?"

I laughed. "Maybe. I plan to find out tonight."

"Your hot date."

I stood, feeling oddly irritated. The heat was becoming suffocation. "Strictly work, Dehan."

"You think she'll call?"

"Yeah, she'll call. If my hunch is right, she has a direct link to Tammy."

"So you think Tammy is still alive?"

"Not necessarily, no. She might be. It's anybody's guess. But my hunch is, whether she is dead or alive, Emma is the link back to whatever it was Tammy was doing two years ago, and our mysterious Southern belle."

"And dos Santos?"

"My bet is he is looking for her too. He is Baxter's client, and Baxter is onto Emma."

"So we are back to the eternal question. Dos Santos employed Tammy to do a job. She screwed him somehow and made off to see Steve. Now dos Santos wants restitution or revenge or both."

"It should be theft."

"You mean he employed her to steal something from Duffy?" She thought about it a moment. "This dame of yours is married to an antiques dealer."

I made a "that's my point" face, but then added, "Only Duffy swears she took nothing." I glanced at my watch. "I'd better get going."

She followed me down to my car. Hers was parked a little farther down, but she hadn't brought her jacket or her keys. Evening was closing in and making long shadows among the russet light. The heat was turning from muggy to sultry. She stood with her hands in her pockets, watching me open the car door and throw my stuff in the back.

"Stone. I'm sorry I got mad at you."

"No. You were right. I should have kept you in the loop."

"You're kind of maddening sometimes, in a nice way."

I smiled. "You're not. In a nice way."

She gave a feeble smile back. "Don't do anything I wouldn't do."

"That should give me a fair bit of scope, then, huh?"

She shook her head. "Not really."

EIGHTEEN

When I got home, I made myself a steak sandwich and poured a generous glass of Irish. Then I sat at the computer and put in a couple of hours' research. There was something nagging at my mind, and I wanted to confirm it. As I ate and drank, and worked my way through the endless pages my searches dredged up, it all slowly began to make sense. One after another, the missing pieces began to slot into place. All except one.

Her call came at eleven p.m., pretty much when I expected it.

"Detective Stone . . . John, it's Emma."

"I know."

"I need . . ." A sigh, loud enough for me to hear, and then she started again. "You were right. I do need you. How did you know? How could you have known? We need to talk. Can I come over?"

"Where are you? It's late."

"At home, on Madison Avenue."

"This isn't Madison Avenue, baby. This is the Bronx."

"You make it sound so . . ."

"It is. Get a taxi. You have my address."

I hung up before she could answer.

It was almost midnight when I heard the distinctive sound of a yellow cab outside. The door slammed like a gunshot in the dark, quiet street. Heels tapped at a half run, and my doorbell rang. I counted slowly to thirty before I got up and went to answer it. I stood blocking the way, looking down at her.

"I thought you weren't coming. I was going to bed."

"My husband . . . Look, I'm here now, aren't I?"

I stood aside and let her in.

She stood, uncertain, in the middle of the floor. I watched her a moment, then reached out my hand. "Give me your coat."

She slipped it off and handed it to me. She was wearing a short, tight black dress that showed off all her curves. They were all the right size and in the right places. She was to celibacy what bacon is to vegetarianism. She said, "Thank you," like it was a meek apology.

I checked the pockets and the lining of her coat. She watched me do it, frowning. I threw the coat on the sofa and went and stood really close to her. "I have to be sure you're not wearing a wire . . ."

I put my hands around her waist and ran them slowly up her sides and over her back and ass. Her breath shuddered. I smiled. It wasn't a friendly smile.

"Don't get the wrong idea, babe. I am just being careful. You want a drink?"

She nodded. I fixed her a martini, extra dry, and poured myself another Irish. She sat on the sofa. I handed her her glass and sat in my armchair. She sipped and looked at me reproachfully.

"You're not being very friendly."

"I want you to be clear, I am not a sap that you can play like your husband. You're as hot as a Carolina reaper, and I'd like nothing better than to take what you're offering, Emma, whether you're offering it or not. But before we get close and cozy, you are going to understand. I don't need you. You didn't get to me. And I will walk away from you the moment you stop being useful."

Her cheeks flushed with anger. I didn't think she could look any more desirable, and right then it was all I could do to keep up my facade of cool indifference. Her voice came as a hiss. "You bastard . . ."

"You're beginning to get the idea."

"I came to you for help!"

"So tell me what you need, and I'll tell you how much it's going to cost you."

She put her drink down. "You really expect me to sit here and put up with this?"

"Yeah, I do. And the sooner you realize I'm not going to be suckered into being your Sir Galahad, the better. Now, what's the deal?"

Tears sprang into her eyes, and she looked away. After a moment, she picked up her drink and took a hefty pull, then started to talk.

"I was born in England . . ."

"That's not news, Emma."

"Just *shut up*, John! Just stop talking and try to stop being quite so *vile*, will you? I am telling you, so just *shut up* and listen!"

She'd finished her drink. She thrust her glass at me, and while I went to refill it, she started talking again.

"My parents weren't rich, but we were comfortably off. We had a comfortable home in Chichester, in West Sussex. My father was a successful solicitor, what you would call an attorney, and my mother stayed at home to look after us . . ."

"Us?"

She was silent for a moment, staring into her drink. "Myself and my sister. We were happy. My father's great passion was sailing. Most weekends we would take the yacht out and sail to the Isle of Wight, or down the coast toward Portsmouth."

She had become drawn and pale.

I allowed some humanity into my voice and asked, "What happened?"

"I was six, my sister was only five. The weather in England is very unpredictable. It was early September, and we had set out early in the morning. The sea was like a sheet of glass. There was a moderate breeze, and the sun was shining." She smiled. "It was a glorious day, and we were all very happy. Mummy had packed a lovely luncheon, and Daddy was in good form, joking and laughing.

"We were a few miles off the Isle of Wight, headed out into the open channel, when there was a severe weather warning over the radio. Very shortly after that, the weather began to change. We weren't worried. We had been in storms before. Daddy was a very good seaman, and so was my mother, for that matter. My sister and I were packed below to play cards, and Daddy set a course back to the Chichester Channel. I remember they were talking about having a heartwarming pint at the pub in Dell Quay when we arrived." She sipped her drink. "Only we never made it to Dell Quay. I don't know what happened. I can only go by what I heard. We were tacking in toward the Chichester Harbor, and as we were coming about, one of the sheets got caught. My mother went to release it but failed to lash herself to the rail. We were struck by a large wave and she was swept overboard. It happened in a matter of seconds."

She stopped talking. She gave a small shrug. It was an eloquent gesture that said it just didn't make any sense.

"I heard my father scream. We saw him scramble past the hatch. We never heard him fall in. The noise of the storm was awful. That was it. We sat there as the storm battered the boat, knocking it sideways to the wind. We were lucky not to be capsized. It was a miracle really.

"We were seen by another yacht also heading in for port. They radioed the lifeboat, and somehow they managed to tow us in to safety. Their bodies were never found."

"Why are you telling me this?"

She spoke into her drink. Her voice was bitter. "Forgive me if I am boring you."

"I didn't say that."

"My sister and I went into care and were put up for adoption. Very few families will take two children. I was adopted by a very loving couple in Surrey. I suppose I never did forgive them for not taking my sister. I think I cried more the day she and I were separated than when my parents died. For a while, they used to take me to visit her, but shortly after that, she was adopted too, by an American family." She heaved a big sigh. "It's a lot for a little six-year-old to take in, John. A lot of loss to assimilate when you are that small. I didn't cry the day they took her away to the airport. I tried to stay strong for her. But something had died inside me."

I knew the answer, but I asked anyway. "Where did they take her?"

"To San Francisco."

"Tamara Gunthersen was your sister?"

"Tamara is my sister."

"She's still alive?"

She nodded.

"Where?"

She faced me and she looked haggard. Her sleek beauty had been replaced by drawn, gray despair. "John, I am desperate. I need help. I will do anything, just name it, anything you want. But for God's sake, you have to help us."

"We'll come to that. First, what is the trouble you're in? And second, where is Tamara?"

She stood and walked to the window. She parted the drapes a little and looked out at the black street.

"She contacted me a couple of years ago. She was very excited. She said she'd been offered a job. She called it a gig. She was an actress, and I assumed it was a part in a play or something. I was used to her getting overexcited; she had been going off the rails a bit ever since our parents died. She was always too happy, too excited, too positive. As though she was trying to convince herself, make herself believe that life wasn't really the black nightmare it had become, that she hadn't really been robbed of every shred of love she had ever been given."

"What happened?"

She turned back to face me. "She said she'd met some billionaire, Hugh Duffy. Old money." She gave an ironic smile. "What you call old money over here. They were in love, and he had asked her to marry him. I was thrilled for her, obviously. But next thing, she phoned me and she was talking crazy. She seemed hyper, hysterical—she was going to New York because she had to square things with Steve."

"Her ex-boyfriend, the loser from the Bronx."

She nodded. "She was always fascinated by him." She gave me a look that was hard to interpret. "This strange attraction bastards have for some women. I told her not to be stupid. She had struck it lucky. Not only did she really seem to love this Hugh character, but he was loaded and seemed to be a genuinely nice man. But she insisted she knew what she was doing, and she came to New York."

She ran her fingers through her hair and flopped into the chair opposite me.

"It was like that bloody storm all over again. One minute, everything was light and sunshine, and the next, all hell had broken loose. She was on the phone to me, hysterical, sobbing her poor little eyes out. She had done something terrible; there were men hunting for her who wanted to kill her . . ."

"What had she done that was so terrible?"

She studied my face a long time. I studied hers back. It was expressionless, hard, calculating.

"She had stolen something."

"From Duffy."

She didn't answer. "She had taken something that she should not have taken, and now there were men after her, who were prepared to kill her in order to get it back."

"What had she stolen?"

"I can't tell you."

"If you want my help, sister . . ."

"I *can't* tell you!" She snapped it and stared at me, hard. "I *cannot* tell you! Don't ask! You don't need to know. The point is, she took it, and these men are after her, and they *will* kill her, not just to get it back, but to make an example of her."

I narrowed my eyes. "Are you talking about Duffy, or are you talking about dos Santos?"

She put her glass down and buried her face in her hands. "Dos Santos is a very, very dangerous man, John. He is pure evil." She looked up at me. "You think you are hard and ruthless, but this man has no soul. He will stop at *nothing*. There is no point beyond which he will not go."

"So what did you do?"

"What could I do? I came to New York. Fortunately, I had good friends here. I was involved in the antiques trade in London, so it wasn't hard for me to find work here. I took Tammy in, made her safe. I met Ulrich, my husband, and we have had an almost normal life until now."

"Tammy lives with you?"

"No. And please don't ask me where she is. I can't and I won't tell you."

"How do you expect me to help you if you don't tell me what she stole or where she is?"

She closed her eyes. "I shouldn't have come here."

"Wrong. Don't go to pieces on me, Emma. For once you made the right choice—stay with it."

She stood. "I need to go home. If Ulrich wakes up . . ."

I stood and moved toward her. I grabbed her by the arms and dragged her close, pressing her hard against me. "Stay! You can't leave it like this! You know I will come after you!"

"John, please . . . !" Her face was barely an inch from mine. Her lips were tender and pink, and her eyes, deep blue, were searching mine for something. I don't know if she found it, but she placed a hand gently on my chest and whispered. "This has been hard for me. I have never told anybody what I have told you tonight. Give me time. I will come back, I promise, and then . . ."

I growled, "And then what?"

"Then, I promise, I will share everything with you. Call me a taxi, John, please . . ."

Five minutes later, I walked her to the cab. Just before she got in, she planted a real, tender kiss on my cheek. And then she was gone. All there was was a pair of red taillights fading into the night.

NINETEEN

I WENT INSIDE AND PHONED DEHAN.

"Do you know what time it is, Stone?"

"One twenty. Were you sleeping?"

"No, I was hanging on the phone, waiting for you to call."

She didn't sound sleepy. "You want a drink?"

"*Now?*"

"I need to tell you what happened."

"And it can't wait till the morning?"

I thought about it. "I'm confused."

She was quiet for a moment. "Sensei is confused. Must be pretty complex."

"It's pretty complex, and I am having trouble telling the lies from the truth."

"Okay."

"Shall I come over?"

I heard her sigh, then the sound of a computer being switched off. "No, I'll come to you."

I dropped a couple of rocks of ice in my whiskey and went and sat on my stoop. Somewhere I could hear the repetitive sawing, croaking of frogs. The air was close and humid, and I took one of the rocks from my drink and rubbed it around the back of my neck, running through in my mind everything that Emma had told me, examining each point, trying to decide which bits were true and which bits were lies.

Dehan arrived twenty minutes later. She pulled up behind my Jag, climbed out, and stood looking at me from the sidewalk.

"How many of those have you had?"

"This is my third."

"I've got some catching up to do, then."

I smiled. It was a relief to see her. Even when she was mad, she was never judgmental. She kept it real.

"You going to come in, or do I have to go and get you?"

She pushed through the gate and came up the path on her long legs and walked past me into the house. I followed. She stood in the middle of the living room, taking in the scene with a cop's eyes: the martini glass half-finished on the floor by the sofa. She turned to face me. "You've got lipstick on your cheek."

"And only on my cheek. Stop jumping to conclusions. You want ice?"

"Yeah. Can we sit in the garden?"

We took our drinks outside and sat at the garden table. The frogs were louder out there. She put her foot on my chair and asked me, "So what happened?"

"She called at eleven . . ." I paused and looked at her. "You have to understand something, I am presenting myself to this woman as a bent cop. So my behavior is not exactly exemplary, okay?"

She gave a small smile, but most of her humor was in her eyes. "Okay . . ."

I told her the whole story, in detail, without leaving anything out. It was almost like a confession, and I was aware while I was doing it that I was looking for some kind of absolution from her.

She listened in silence, holding her glass in both hands and watching me. When I'd finished, she gave a small sigh and sipped her drink. Then she gave a small laugh. "You called her *babe*?"

I snorted. "I guess I was inspired by your talk of Frisco and yeggs." I became serious. "The point is, I am having trouble telling the truth from fantasy here."

She was quiet for a long while, turning her glass in her fingers. After a bit, she asked me the question that was eating her. "Stone, is she getting to you?"

"What do you mean?"

She fixed me with her big black eyes. "We can be straight with each other, right? I have to tell you, you have been acting strange since you met her. Are you falling for her?"

"Of course not."

"There is no 'of course' about it, Stone. You said yourself this woman is beautiful. She is intense and passionate. Hell, she sounds fascinating. Any man would be attracted to her."

"I am not falling for her, Dehan."

She shrugged. "Okay, whatever you say. So what is it that's confusing you?"

I frowned. "The whole thing sounds fantastic. The two sisters separated. One is brought to the States. The other is brought up in England. The younger one falls in with a guy who is 'pure evil' and 'has no soul.' It's like a Mexican soap opera. Now she has her hidden and can't tell me where she is. All the cloak-and-dagger mystery." I sat forward and put my elbows on my knees. "I'll tell you, before she arrived and told me her crazy story, I was convinced I had it sewn up. Now I don't know what to believe."

She drained her glass, stood, and went inside. She came out with the bottle and refilled my glass and her own.

"I'll replace this tomorrow," she said, and sat. "You want my advice?" I nodded. "Bring her in."

"What?"

"Come on, Stone. It's as clear as daylight. If it was anybody else, you wouldn't think twice about it."

"I can get more out of her if I play her along."

"Bullshit. We have an eyewitness who saw Tamara Gunthersen commit a double homicide, and she may well have been party to a third. Emma Girt is harboring a suspected murderer. Bring her in and throw the book at her. Threaten her with jail time if she doesn't give up the whereabouts of her sister. Make her understand that if she does not cooperate, her husband, her business, and her million-dollar lifestyle on Madison Avenue are going to go up in smoke."

She watched me and read my face like a book. I puffed out my cheeks and blew hard. She pointed at me. "Now you need to be asking yourself, what makes her different? Because you and I both know, if it was anybody else, you would be all over them like a rash. So what makes this dame different?"

I thought about it.

"Nothing."

"So?"

"I am not protecting her."

"So what *are* you doing?"

I spread my hands. "I'm trying to understand, Dehan. This woman is hiding a lot of secrets. If we go charging in like a bull in a china shop, we risk her clamming up and blowing our one shot at this case. I am not convinced that her million-dollar lifestyle on Madison Avenue is all that important to her."

"You think her aspirations are more spiritual?"

"Don't be sarcastic."

"Sorry. Let me ask you something, Stone."

"What?"

"Why did you ask me to come here tonight?"

I shrugged. "I value your . . ."

"No. Not all that. Why did *you* ask me here. Why did you ask somebody, anybody, to come here tonight."

I frowned. "Because I was confused. I needed to . . ."

She cut across me. "When was the last time you were this kind of confused about a case?"

She had me pinned like a bug on a board. I stared at her a long time. "Never."

She raised her eyebrows and said, "So here is the John Stone classic question. What is it about this case that makes it so much more confusing than any other? And you and I both know the answer."

"Her."

"You said it yourself, Stone, you had the whole thing clear in your head until she showed up and started putting lipstick on your cheek. And only on your cheek. Let me ask you another question, partner."

I sighed. "What?"

"When was the last time you got laid?"

"That is none of your goddamn business."

"Are you sure?"

"My sexual frustration, assuming I have any, is not affecting my professional judgment, Dehan!"

"But your lust for this woman—and I am assuming that is all it is, Stone—may be. I sure as hell hope you are not falling in love with her."

I drained my glass and put it on the table.

"Let's get something clear for once and for all, Dehan. I am not in love with Emma. I am not lusting after Emma." I nodded several times. "Yes, she has thrown me a curveball. Whether she has done it deliberately or whether there is some other reason, I don't know. But my judgment is not impaired by lust or love. Are we clear?"

She shook her head. "No. I'll take your word for it, and I trust you, but I am not clear on either of those two points. And make no mistake, I am going to be watching you like a hawk. Now, I am giving you my advice. Haul her in and put her on the rack."

I thought about it a long time. In the end I shook my head.

"Watch me. Like you said, watch me like a hawk. If you see me making a seriously bad move, jump on me. But right now, I know we can get a lot more from her if I play along. She said she'd come back and share everything with me. If she does, we may get not just Tammy but Geronimo too. Let's wait."

She sighed. She wasn't happy, but she agreed. She nodded and said, "Okay, Stone, but stop scaring me, will you?"

I laughed. "I can't promise the impossible, Dehan. One for the road?"

"Come on, then. One for the road."

We toasted and drank. She smacked her lips and sighed, with that inscrutable smile she had sometimes.

"Guess I'm the lucky one, then."

"How's that?"

"She drives you crazy, but I get to stay the night."

I chuckled. "*And* you cook me breakfast."

"What woman does that for you, Stone?"

"Nobody. Only you, Dehan."

"That's what I'm sayin'."

TWENTY

We didn't have to wait long. Next morning, as we were releasing Peter Gunthersen, at about half ten, my phone rang. It was Emma.

"John, we need to talk."

"Wait." I signaled Dehan with my eyebrows and took myself outside. "What is it?"

"I haven't slept all night."

"I didn't sleep a lot myself."

"You have upset everything. I don't know if I am coming or going."

"I'm at work. I can't talk a lot. What's on your mind?"

"I have to see you."

"Tonight."

"No. Now."

"What for? I told you I'm at work."

"It's urgent, John. I told you our lives are at risk."

I made a show of thinking about it.

"Where?"

"At your house."

"This better be worth it, Emma. I don't aim to play any games with you."

"I'll make it worth your while, I promise . . ."

"You know you will. Give me an hour."

"I'll be there."

Dehan was watching me from the doorway. I walked back to her.

"She wants to see me in an hour, at my place. Go find Baxter. If he's not there, wait for him. Bring him in. Hold him. Don't let him see a lawyer—delay him, bullshit him, do whatever you have to do. Threaten him with a charge of conspiracy to murder. I want an address for dos Santos."

She nodded. "Okay."

She went inside and I headed home, wondering what Emma was going to hit me with this time. I tried to focus on what the case had originally been about. Who murdered Steve Springfellow, and maybe Tamara Gunthersen. But with every clue we unearthed, we seemed to get not just further from an answer, but further from the original question.

I pulled in in front of Dehan's car and sat staring at it, remembering her words the night before. "What is it about this case in particular that makes it so confusing?"

I got out and went inside.

Twenty minutes later, Emma arrived in a cab. I watched her pay the driver, then run across the road. She was carrying a small parcel. I opened the door and let her in.

She didn't say anything. She just put her hand on my chest and stared up into my face. Then she walked inside and put the parcel on the dining table.

"Give me a drink, will you?"

"It's eleven in the morning."

A spasm of anger flashed across her face. "Oh, *fuck that! Just give me a fucking drink, will you!*" She closed her eyes and took a deep, shuddering breath. "My nerves are shot to pieces."

I poured her a shot of whiskey, and she downed it in one. Then she held out the glass for me to refill it. I did. She sipped it and set it down on the table, next to the parcel. I nodded at it.

"What's this?"

"I have had enough, John. Baxter, and then you, crashing into my life, threatening me, forever having to look over my shoulder. I can't. I can't live like this. I want out. I want to take Tammy and get out."

"That's not going to be so easy."

"You think I don't know that?"

"Who did Tamara steal from, Emma?"

She sighed. "Technically, from Hugh Duffy. But as far as dos Santos is concerned, she stole for him, and whatever she stole belongs to him."

"What the hell did she steal?"

"This."

She undid the wrapping to reveal a wooden box, about one foot square and three or four inches deep. She opened the box and extracted a small painting in a fairly plain, gold leaf frame. It was a portrait of a woman. She was in Renaissance dress and had been watching the artist as he worked. She had humorous eyes and very elegant clothes. I studied it a moment, then looked at Emma and shrugged.

She said, "That is Clarice Orsini, the wife of Lorenzo de' Medici, Leonardo da Vinci's patron. It was painted by Leonardo in 1469, just after their marriage. Its value is incalculable."

I raised an eyebrow. "This is an original da Vinci, and you're carrying it around in a box?"

"This is what Tammy stole from Hugh Duffy on Geronimo dos Santos' orders."

I put the painting back in the box. "Why have you brought it here?"

"Because I want you to hold it. I want you to conduct the negotiations. All I ask is that you make it so that dos Santos leaves us alone and we can go back to a normal life. Whatever money you make on the sale, keep for yourself. I want no part of it, and neither does Tammy. All we want is our lives back."

"Slow down, sister." I went and got a glass and poured myself a shot. I took a slug and rested my ass against the back of the armchair. "In the first place, it's not just dos Santos. It's the cops too. Tammy is wanted in connection with two, maybe three murders. And in the second place, what makes you think I'm not just going to take the money and run?"

She pulled out a chair and sat. "John, with what you make from that painting, you will never have to work again as long as you live. You won't just be rich, you will be fabulously rich." She paused, studying my face. "And I am not stupid. I know it would be easy for you to fix it so that suspicion is deflected away from Tammy. Her case went cold through lack of evidence. It can go cold again, or better still, it can get closed. Steve was shot with Pete's revolver; so was Ernesto and so was Danny Schultz. How hard would it be to pin the murders on Peter?" She watched me a moment and then gave a knowing smile. "Or if that troubles your conscience, pin it on Danny, who then got mugged and rained on with his own .38."

She stood and came to me, slipping her silky thigh between my legs and sliding her hands over my chest. "And what you get in return is more money than you can imagine in your wildest dreams . . . and anything else you want." I didn't respond, and she smiled. "The answer to your second question is that I can see right through that tough facade to the real man inside. I know what you want, John Stone, and so do you. You want me." She pushed herself away from me and returned to the table. "Of course, if you're not interested . . ."

I smiled. "You know I am, babe. But this has to be done right. Can you contact dos Santos?"

She nodded. "Yes, I know how to get a message to him."

"I don't want Baxter involved."

She shook her head. "He won't be involved."

"But getting him off your back is not going to be easy. He will want to punish Tammy. He has to punish Tammy to make an example of her."

She nodded. "I know. I've thought of that. If, between us, we can get enough information on him to incriminate him, the deal would be, he buys back his painting—he isn't paying anyway, so he won't care—and we don't use the information against him."

"What do you mean, he isn't paying? If he isn't, who is?"

"His master in Galicia, in Spain. Cardinal Guzman. Ultimately, the Vatican."

"Sweet. So how do we get this information?"

She smiled and her eyes seemed to sparkle with an unholy light. "You gave me the idea last night. We arrange a negotiation. You are there as my muscle and my representative. But you wear a wire. Ostensibly, we are there to negotiate, but in reality, we are there to gather information."

I nodded. "It might work."

"Oh, John! It will work, I know it will! And think, when it is all over, you will be rich! We can . . ." She faltered. "I'm sorry . . ."

"Not yet, Emma. Let's stay focused. Then we'll see what happens."

She looked down into her drink. "You probably hate me anyway."

"Probably."

She looked up at me. I smiled. After a moment, she smiled back.

"Tammy worries me. She sounds like a loose cannon. I want to meet her and talk to her. Today. Then you set up the meeting with dos Santos." I stood. "You better go, and I need to get back to the precinct. Fix it with Tammy and call me."

She stood. She hesitated a moment, then took two quick steps and clung to me. "John, thank you. I have been so scared. I am so grateful . . ."

I held her face in my hands and looked into her eyes. "There will be plenty of time for gratitude later, Emma. For now, let's stay focused. This is not going to be easy."

"I know."

Her body was warm and soft, and every instinct in me was telling me to give in and take what she was offering. But I knew that would be as good as suicide, and I wasn't ready for that quite yet. She reached up and kissed me on the cheek again, then said, "Let me just use your loo," and she trotted up the stairs with her purse.

I gathered up the glasses and took them to the kitchen, then I called her a cab. Two minutes later she was down again, smiling.

I watched her drive away. I felt troubled. We were moving forward, but where to? She was playing a subtle game, that much was obvious, but whose game?

I went inside and put some coffee on. While it was brewing, I went upstairs to have a shower and clear my head. While I was stripping off my shirt, I saw it on the floor, behind the toilet. It was a package, maybe six or seven inches square and three inches deep. It looked like it had fallen out of her purse while she was using what she called the loo. It was gift wrapped and tied with a bow, but there was no name tag on it.

I picked up my cell and called her.

"John, what is it?"

"You left a gift behind."

"What?" There was a pause. I could hear her rummaging. "Oh, damn! It's Tammy's birthday tomorrow. It's just a silly gift. Can you hang on to it for me and give it to me when we meet later?"

"Sure."

"Thank you, darling."

She hung up.

I put the package on my bed and stepped into the shower.

TWENTY-ONE

After my shower, I did a few things I needed to do, then went downstairs feeling better. I poured myself some coffee and called Dehan. She sounded relieved to hear from me.

"How'd it go?"

"It went well. I'll tell you about it when we meet. How about you?"

"He's not in his office, and I've been sitting here all morning watching the damn place. He hasn't shown."

"Okay, I'll come over. We need to talk. Then we'll decide what to do about Baxter."

Half an hour later, I pulled up on Melrose Avenue, a few cars behind Dehan's unmarked vehicle. I walked up and she lowered the window.

"No sign?"

She shook her head. It felt wrong, and all the way there, in the car, I'd been getting more edgy. There were alarm bells going off everywhere, but I couldn't see the cause. I glanced over at the street entrance, then up at his window, like I had Superman's X-ray vision and I could somehow see inside his office. I couldn't. I gave the roof of her car a couple of gentle thumps and said, "Let's go up."

She got out and we dodged through the traffic. Then we rode the slow, ancient elevator from the dark lobby up to the top floor. His door was locked. I listened.

"Do you hear that?"

She grinned. "What, a woman crying for help? That's not going to work here, Stone."

I shook my head. "No, the fan. The electric fan is still on." I sniffed the air. There was everything from carbon monoxide and furniture polish to boiled cabbage and bacon, all the smells of a city. But there was something else too. I pulled out my piece and shot out the lock. It's the quickest way known to man of opening a door.

Baxter was at his desk. He was sitting back, watching us as we walked in. His electric fan ruffled his hair as it made another relentless sweep of his office, but he didn't feel it. His mouth was open and his eyes were staring, but he wasn't breathing or seeing. Decay had set in, and the smell was pretty bad. There were already flies swarming over the big wound in his chest. For them, his death was not a problem, it was an opportunity. I wondered if Baxter had anybody to mourn him.

I pulled out my cell and called the 43rd.

"This is Stone. We need a meat wagon and crime scene team at Melrose and 154th. Notify the ME too."

Dehan was over by the door, examining the bits of lock and wood that had been punched out by my slug. "I can't find the key," she said, and then, after a moment, "He's sitting down. You notice the first time we came to see him, he got up to greet us? Whoever came in, he was familiar enough with them not to feel the need." She stood. "They just walked in, pulled a gun, shot him, took the key, and locked him in."

I nodded. "Sounds about right."

"Tamara?"

I shrugged. "Maybe."

"She heard through Emma that Baxter was onto her, so she came and shot him."

"That would mean that Baxter was familiar with Tamara."

"So that leaves Emma, dos Santos, or one of his men."

"We'll have to wait and see what the ME says. My money is on a .38. But the fact is that with an operator like Baxter, this could have been any one of a dozen people."

My cell rang. It was Emma. I showed Dehan the screen and answered.

"Yeah."

"Stone, it's me. I've arranged it. I'm at my beach house at Napeague Park, on Long Island. Geronimo will be here at nine. Can you be here for eight?"

"Napeague Park? That's at the easternmost tip. It's a three-hour drive."

"I know, darling. I thought, when it's all over, we could spend a couple of days here, just you and me . . ."

My mind was racing ahead of me. I spoke mechanically, without thinking. "That sounds nice, baby, but I told you, we'll have time to discuss that afterward. First we attend to business."

"I know, darling. Say you'll be here."

"I'll be there. What about Tamara? I told you I wanted to meet her first."

"That's why I want you here at eight. She'll be here."

"Will dos Santos be alone?"

"No, he goes everywhere with Ronaldo, his gorilla."

"Okay, I'll see you at eight."

"And, darling?"

"What?"

"Be armed. These men are dangerous."

"Leave that to me."

I hung up. Dehan was watching me with a face like a hanging judge who just sat on a wasp.

"You want to tell me what's going down at Napeague Park, baby?"

"A meeting, with Geronimo, Tamara, and Emma." I told her about the portrait and the deal she wanted to make. "We need to get a wire fixed up, and backup. And we need to run this by the captain."

She nodded. "Go. I'll wait for the team and the ME. You need to leave here at four thirty or you're going to hit the rush hour. You haven't got long. I'll be at the briefing before you go."

"Okay." I turned to go.

As I reached the door, she said, "Stone?"

I stopped. "Yeah?"

"Be careful, baby."

"Take a hike."

I glanced at my watch as I climbed in my car. It was almost half one. I drove fast back to the precinct and sprinted up the stairs to the captain's office. I knocked and went in without waiting for a reply. He looked up at me and removed his reading glasses in a way that said he was being patient because I was usually worth it.

I sat without being invited to do so.

"Captain, I need a wire and I need two cars out at Napeague Park. I also need the harbor patrol alerted, and I need it all in place by tonight at eight o'clock."

He heaved a big sigh. "It's never a simple arrest with you, is it, Stone?"

I shrugged. "Cold cases are cold because they are not simple, sir."

He nodded. It was a reluctant nod. "Okay, Stone, run me through it."

DEHAN GOT BACK AT THREE. I was fitted with the wire and tested, and then we had the briefing with the two backup teams. One would be concealed off Dunes Lane, two hundred yards from the house. The other would be off the Montauk Highway. Both vehicles would be unmarked off-road SUVs capable of driving over dunes. Additionally, the harbor patrol had agreed to dispatch a launch to that area of the beach. Nobody was getting away from me that night.

At three forty-five, Dehan and the backup cars set off to take up their positions as inconspicuously as possible. I watched them leave and climbed into my Jag. As I put the key in the ignition, my cell rang. The caller ID was withheld.

"Detective Stone."

"Detective Stone, it is a pleasure to speak to you." If voices had colors, this one would have been green and slimy. "My name is Geronimo dos Santos. We are due to meet later this evening. I wonder if we could have a little, private chat beforehand."

"What's on your mind?"

He laughed like I was not so much funny, as amusing. "Not over the phone, my dear fellow. No, come and see me at my hotel. We will have a civilized drink and a chat, and then we can each make our way to the meeting with Emma, at the beach house."

"Give me one good reason why I should."

He was silent for a moment. When he spoke, you could tell he was smiling. He still found me amusing. "Let us say that there are things about our hostess that you should know, before you commit yourself to this negotiation on her behalf. All you need to do, Detective, is listen to me. If you find I do not convince you, then we proceed as arranged. What have you to lose?"

I thought about it for a moment. "Where are you?"

"At the Plaza, on Fifth Avenue, in the Royal Suite."

"I'll be there in twenty minutes."

I headed for the Bruckner Expressway and called Dehan as I went.

"Yeah, what's up?"

"Dos Santos just called me."

"He did?"

"Yeah. He wants a meeting before the meeting. I'm going to see him at the Plaza."

"What do you want us to do?"

"Go ahead as planned. I'll keep you posted if anything changes."

"Okay."

I parked on West 58th and made my way on foot to the Grand Army Plaza. When I asked the receptionist how to get to the Royal Suite, he raised a skeptical eyebrow at me that was rich with pseudo nineteenth-century grandeur.

"Are you Detective Stone?" He asked it in a generic French accent.

"Yeah."

"'E is expecting you."

He directed me toward the elevators. I rode up to the suite, wondering why all hotel receptionists pretended to be French.

The door to the Royal Suite was opened by something an anthropologist would have wanted to preserve and study. He was dressed in an Italian suit, but you could tell he missed his furs.

"Stone. I'm here to see dos Santos."

He would have frowned, only that's hard to do with only one eyebrow. He jerked his head, indicating I should come in, and led the way to a room that looked like a set from *Downton Abbey*. Geronimo dos Santos was fat. He had enough chins for a large family. He was sitting at a dark mahogany dining table that Emma would have approved of, with a bottle of champagne in a silver ice bucket by his side. He had a plate and a silver bowl in front of him, and he was stuffing his face with caviar and crackers. He glanced at me as I came in but didn't say anything.

Ape Man pulled out a chair for me and indicated with his hand that I should sit. Speaking was obviously not the big thing around here. I was about to tell dos Santos I was short of time when he spoke suddenly.

"Some people," he said, "believe it should be eaten with vodka. But in my opinion, those people are brutish. Caviar has a rich spectrum of subtle flavors. Vodka numbs our palate, so we perceive only a fraction of those delicate tones. No." He shook his head. "We want the clean, delicate flavors of a Krug Clos d'Ambonnay, to sensitize our palate to receive the exquisite taste of the roe."

"Spare me your bullshit, dos Santos. What do you want?"

He looked at me with distaste, like I was spoiling his lunch by wearing the wrong aftershave.

"You have somewhere else to be, Detective?"

"Yeah, and you have five seconds to start saying something I find interesting. If you don't, this interview is over."

He sighed and reached for the bottle. I could tell he was counting out the seconds as he refilled his glass. On six, he said, "Can I offer you a drink? I hate to drink alone."

I stood. He held up a hand.

"Detective, you are not the only man with a busy schedule. I have no desire to waste your time, let alone my own. If I have asked you here, it is because I think we can both benefit. Please, have a drink and allow me to explain."

I sat. "Spare me the lessons on how to eat my caviar, and get to the point."

He turned to Ape Man. "Ronaldo, get the detective a drink." He turned to me. "I am guessing you are a whiskey man, Detective Stone."

"Bushmills, no ice."

Ronaldo disappeared and dos Santos spooned caviar onto a cracker and stuffed it in his mouth.

"Who has the . . ." He hesitated for a second. "Who has the box, Detective?"

"I have."

"Have you looked inside?"

"How is that any of your business?"

He looked at me with a face that could have skinned a rabbit. "Because I am paying a substantial sum of money for it. Have you looked inside the box?"

I lied and said, "No. Emma advised me not to."

He raised an eyebrow and nodded. After a moment, he said, "You realize that Emma is quite mad."

"And what, are you quite sane?"

He sighed. "You are a difficult man to talk to, Stone. We are not making progress."

"I get antsy when people bullshit me. Why don't you get to the point, dos Santos?"

Ronaldo came in with a silver tray and a crystal tumbler of whiskey on it. I took a sip. I was beginning to feel I needed it.

"The point I am trying to make, Stone, is that she may have misled you as to the real value of the contents of the box."

I laughed. "Oh, really? So this elaborate circus you have going on here—the Krug, the caviar, Baxter, and the two years you have been hunting for Tamara Gunthersen—that is all over something that is really of very little value at all."

He gave a breathless little chortle. "By no means, Detective. I mean that she may have misled you into believing it is *less* valuable than it really is."

I frowned.

"She is quite mad. And I, and the people I represent, would be willing to be very generous friends, Detective Stone, if you would cooperate with us. Let me explain what I have in mind."

He held out his glass, as though proposing a toast. I was keen to hear, and record, what he had to say. So I knocked his glass with mine, and we both drank. I couldn't work out at first why he was smiling. He turned to Ronaldo, who was now also smiling, and in a voice that sounded like it was all the way across the room, he said, "Get the car ready, Ronaldo. I think Detective Stone is just about ready."

I tried to swear, but my brain had stopped talking to my mouth and all that came out was a slur. I tried to stand, but that didn't work either, because the table rose up and hit me in the face. And then there was nothing.

TWENTY-TWO

THE FIRST THING I WAS AWARE OF WAS A SHARP PAIN IN my shoulders that was making it hard to breathe. Then I realized the pain was in my wrists and arms, and also in my ankles and my legs. I felt sick too.

I opened my eyes and slowly focused. It didn't make much difference because the room was dark. A horizontal crack of light slowly resolved itself into a window with the blind drawn down. Another, farther away and at an odd angle, became a door. And as I slowly adjusted to the feelings in my body, I realized I was sitting, not lying, and I was tightly bound to a chair with duct tape. Usually, being bound to a chair is not a good sign.

I tried to clear my head and hollered at the door a few times. After the third shout, it opened and the Thing came in and looked at me.

"You awake?"

"No, I'm deeply asleep and you are part of my dream. That's why you are in here." He tried to work it out, but it's hard when you only have one eyebrow. "Just tell Geronimo to get his fat ass in here and untie me!"

He gave a nod and went away, down some stairs that were just out of sight. Slowly, my brain functions were coming back. I listened hard to see if I could get some clue as to where I was. The silence was almost total, but there was something like white noise just in my peripheral hearing.

Surf. I was at the beach house, then.

I heard two sets of feet climbing heavily up stairs. There was also the heavy breathing of a man carrying too much weight. Geronimo entered the room and flipped a switch. I winced in the sudden glare but took in a writing desk and a chair, a gray carpet, and a bare white wall. Geronimo was leaning on the desk catching his breath. Ronaldo, proto-man, was standing in front of me looking like evolution gone wrong. Geronimo heaved a breath and gave a small laugh.

"I am not as young as I was. There was a time I would have sprinted up those stairs. And I try to observe a healthy diet, but age, Stone. It comes to us all, and it does not forgive."

Here we were, a couple of pals having a chat. He pulled out the chair and lowered himself onto it.

"Now, Stone, where is the box?"

"Go fuck yourself."

"Very well. Ronaldo, I think six should do."

It was like getting hit by a wall. I weigh two hundred and twenty pounds, and he made the chair rock. By the second blow, I was disoriented and wondering how I was going to get through another four. He made it easy for me by delivering three of them to my chest, so I felt like I had a rusty saw stuck through my lungs. The last was a backhander that left the room spinning and my ears ringing.

Through the pain, I heard dos Santos' voice.

"Now, let us at least dispense with the vulgarities, Stone. Perhaps I had better apprise you of the situation. Your wire has been removed. Detective Dehan has received a text message instructing her to stand down and await further instructions from you. So nobody is going to come charging to your rescue. You have one chance of survival and one only. Tell me where the box is, and where Tammy is."

I knew I had to think. Somehow I had to get my brain working, but Ronaldo's beating had left me groping for consciousness. I played for time, exaggerating my grogginess. I didn't have to try very hard.

"You're out of your fucking mind. You think I am stupid enough to make it this easy for you?"

"Frankly? I do, yes. I don't want to resort to mutilation, Stone, but if you try my patience, Ronaldo here is pretty handy with a pair of pliers. Don't push your luck. If I don't have an answer in the next ten minutes, one of you starts losing digits, or some other parts of the anatomy which may be more persuasive."

I looked up at Ronaldo's passive face. It held the kind of peace only stupidity can bring. I looked past him at Geronimo. He was smiling. I knew I had to turn the situation around pretty soon, or I was going to be in big trouble.

"I don't know where Tamara is, but you and I both know, dos Santos, that if I give you the box, I will be dead within seconds. Now you must be aware that I am too smart and too experienced to put myself in that situation."

He looked complacent. "I just don't think you have had enough time to do anything other than put it somewhere safe." He gave a small laugh. "In fact, I am not even totally convinced that Emma has given it to you."

"I'll tell you where it is, dos Santos. It's in a drawer, in a desk at the 43rd Precinct. Not my desk—the desk of a uniform sergeant who has instructions to put it in the mail if she doesn't hear from me by midnight tonight. Now you can torture an address out of me, but how will you ever know if I have given you the right address?"

"You're bluffing."

"Maybe I am, Geronimo. But again, how will you ever know?"

He struggled to his feet. "Come on, Ronaldo. Let us go and talk to Emma for a while, and see if she can be more cooperative."

They closed the door, and I heard their big feet lumbering

down the stairs. They would question Emma to see if she confirmed or denied what I had told them. So far, I was on safe ground. But I wouldn't be able to keep the game going indefinitely. And I could not rely on Dehan realizing the messages were not from me. At least not for several hours.

Duct tape is a very useful, easy way of immobilizing somebody. It only has one drawback. Rope, especially nylon rope, is hard to cut through. With duct tape, all you need to do is nick it in the right place and it tears right in half. I peered around the room, looking for something with a sharp angle. There was nothing immediately apparent. Then I became aware that just behind me there was a bed. I started rocking the chair from side to side and angling my body so that the chair shifted. Soon I could see, over my shoulder, exactly what I had hoped for. A bedside table with a lamp on it. It was a long shot, but it was worth a try.

I did a little more angling, rocked a couple of times, and then, putting all my weight into one final rock, I threw myself backward onto the lamp. I smacked my head hard against the wall, and the chair got wedged at a forty-five-degree angle over the bedside table. But underneath my wrists and hands, I felt the glass shade of the lamp crack and shatter into shards. One of which I held in my bleeding fingers. It was enough. I moved it around until I had the tip wedged into the edge of the tape. Then I pushed and felt the tape cut. Another couple of slashes, and the pressure from my wrists was enough to do the rest.

With my hands free, I acted quickly, leaning forward and hacking at the tape around my ankles. I stood, unsteadily at first, with my head swimming and a feeling of nausea in my stomach. I moved to the door, opened it a fraction, and listened. There was silence.

There was a landing and, at the far end, a stairwell leading down. Dim light filtered up from below. I moved to the banisters and peered down. There wasn't much to see, a carpeted staircase and part of a hallway. I had no weapon and no phone to call for backup. I took a couple of steps down and peered through the railings. The hallway was a broad space. Ahead of me, I could see the front door. To one side there was another door that was closed but obviously gave onto a room at the front of the house, facing the sea. Next to it, there was an arch, and through it, three broad steps that led down into a large, modern living room. The lights were off, but I could make out a large fireplace with a copper hood, a cream sofa, and a large armchair. But no people. Another couple of steps and I could see that to the right there was a passage, and my gut told me that led to the kitchen.

I slipped into the living room. I was on a mezzanine floor with two steps to a lower level, where one whole wall was made of plate glass, in the middle of which there were two sliding doors that now stood open onto a broad, weatherboard terrace that was bathed in moonlight. Now I could hear voices and the sound of the surf.

Keeping in the shadows, I slipped along the wall to stand in the corner, looking out onto the terrace. They had the terrace lights off and were sitting like moonlit ghosts at a table. Beyond them, I could see the luminous ocean and the lights of a small launch.

Emma spoke suddenly.

"Please, Geronimo, I am begging of you, please don't hurt him. Please, don't hurt him."

Geronimo gave a high-pitched wheeze, which must have been a laugh, and said, "Oh, I am going to hurt him, Emma. I am going to make him weep like a child, and I am going to make you watch every second of it until he dies, sobbing for his mommy. Unless, of course, you tell me where the box is. And where is Tammy?"

TWENTY-THREE

"I am sick of telling you!" Her voice was a hiss in the night, like an echo from the surf on the beach. "*I don't know!* For this very reason, Geronimo! I *knew* that you would try something. I knew that you'd try to trick us and betray us."

He gave a screech like a parrot. "*That!* That is fine! When it was your sister who cheated *me* in the first place! If she had stuck to the terms of our agreement in the first place, we would not *be* in this mess now!"

"An agreement that gave her a filthy two thousand dollars while you netted an incalculable fortune!"

He leaned forward and spat the words viciously at her. "It was not for me! It was for the Mother Church! He had no place owning that treasure! It belongs to the Church!"

"This is getting us nowhere."

"Where is Tamara?"

"Where you can never find her."

"*Where is she!*"

"*Never! I will never tell you!*" They were both silent, glaring at each other. Then Emma exploded, "Why are you so *obsessed* with her? Why can't you let her be?"

"Because she stole from me, and she must pay."

"You are such a *cretin*! If you had just left things as they were, Geronimo! You would have your bloody box! I would have my money and my guarantee, and we would be done! Now you get *nothing*!"

"Fine!" He pounded the table with his fist. "Have it your way! Ronaldo, go and get him!"

Ronaldo moved toward the plate glass doors. As he did so, Emma threw herself at him, clawing at his arm and pleading, "Please! Please don't hurt him! For God's sake, please! Please don't!"

Geronimo pounded the table again. "*Enough of this!*"

"I swear to you he has the box! I gave it to him so that you could not get it from me! *I don't know where it is!* Kill him and you will never get it!"

I stepped out onto the terrace.

"She's telling the truth. She gave it to me this morning, and we agreed she would have no knowledge of what I did with it."

Geronimo gaped. "Stone! What the . . . ?" He glared at Ronaldo and screamed like a hysterical woman. "*You incompetent fool!*"

"Now, you are at an impasse, Geronimo. The clock is ticking. Hurt Emma or hurt me, you will never see the box again. In a week, it could be anywhere in the world. You tried to be too smart. Now, you have one chance and one chance only. Accept you will have to buy the box with more than money."

"What do you mean, more than money?"

"A confession, signed and recorded, that implicates all three of us. If any one of us gets hurt, the other two go down."

"That's absurd!"

"That's the deal. Take it or leave it."

His face went crimson, and he pounded the table with both fists till I thought he was going to have a stroke. Even Ronaldo looked curious.

Dos Santos leaned across the table, pointing a finger just an inch from Emma's face. "Just once! Just once I saw her! Perfect!

Beautiful! Enrapturing! If I could have owned her, I would have bought her! But I knew, I *knew*." Now he pounded the side of his head with his finger. "God spoke to me. 'She is the spawn of the Devil! She will be only trouble!' Five minutes I saw her and I knew!" He dropped back into his chair. "But I was desperate to do God's work, and I was a *fool*!"

"You're a boring man, Geronimo. You talk a lot of shit. Now what's it to be? If we have a deal, let's do it. If there is no deal, Emma and I are walking out of here, and you know there is damn all you can do about it."

Ronaldo pulled his gun and pointed it at me. I looked Geronimo in the eye and said, "You have five seconds to make him put that gun on the table. If he doesn't, I walk. Then one of two things is going to happen. One, you will kill me, and then you will never see your box. Two, you won't kill me, and you will never see your box. You see how it works, Geronimo. Now, I am counting . . ."

Geronimo waved his hand at Ronaldo. "Put down the gun. Put it down."

Ronaldo shrugged like he thought his boss was stupid. He wasn't wrong. He put the gun on the table. I thought what would happen next would be that Emma would hand me the gun, but I guess I was a bit stupid too. Instead, she reached out like she was reaching for a pack of cigarettes. Both Geronimo and Ronaldo frowned at her hand, like they were mildly surprised. She picked it up calmly and deliberately, pointed it at Ronaldo, and shot him in the heart. Then, without losing her composure, she turned it on Geronimo.

He screamed again and threw the table up and over so that it crashed against Emma, knocking her off her chair. Next thing, he was flying at me like a quarterback. He piled into me, ramming me against the wall and knocking all the wind out of me. I fell to the floor gasping, and he was off again, sprinting across the floor with astonishing agility. As I staggered to my feet, Emma scrambled out from under the table. She screamed a scream of pure rage and sprinted past me, after dos Santos.

I made after her, but my lungs were in spasm and my head was reeling. She was up the stairs onto the mezzanine floor, and I heard the front door slam. I followed and she skidded out into the hall. I shouted after her, "*Emma! No!*" But she wasn't listening. She had one thought in her mind and one thought only.

She wrenched open the front door. Outside in the moonlight, I heard a car door slam. On the porch, I saw her straddle her legs and take aim. I heard tires scream, and I hurled myself at her. The gun cracked twice before I collided with her and threw her to the ground.

She clambered to her feet, training the gun on me. Her eyes were wide, and she looked really crazy. I shouted at her, "Are you *crazy? Are you nuts? What have you done?*"

"Stay away from me!"

There was a second car, a Mercedes convertible. She backed toward it, with the gun still trained on me. She climbed in and I watched her fire up the engine and take off at speed after dos Santos.

I stood watching her taillights vanish up the road in the pale moonlight. My head was reeling. We'd had him. What she'd done didn't make any sense.

Unless . . .

I went inside and scoured the house for my gun and my phone. After twenty minutes, I found my gun in Ronaldo's waistband out on the porch. Even now, staring up at the translucent sky, he looked more bemused than surprised. My phone I eventually found in plain sight, sitting on a coffee table in the living room.

The bar was easier to find. I poured myself a stiff whiskey and phoned Dehan.

"Stone! What the hell is happening?"

"Nothing good."

"Why did you stand us down?"

"I didn't. Believe it or not, I was drugged. He took my phone and sent you the message."

"Dos Santos?"

"Yeah, he is one devious son of a bitch."

"Holy shit!"

"Tell me about it. I need you to come and get me. I also need a CSI team and the ME. There has been another homicide. The captain's going to have to liaise with the local precinct."

"Oh, he is going to love you."

"I'm not too fond of me myself, right now. I can't believe I got suckered like that."

"He's a slippery customer."

"They're both as crazy as a box of frogs."

"Okay. I'll be there in a couple of hours."

TWENTY-FOUR

WE GOT HOME TO MY PLACE JUST AFTER FOUR IN THE morning. She sat me at the table and examined the damage.

"Boy, Stone, you look like somebody set fire to your face and put it out with a brick."

"Thanks. You're beautiful too."

"There are no cuts, though. It's just bruises."

"Is that all?"

She nodded. "You must have a pretty hard face."

"Yeah, it's the way I was raised. Every time I was bad, my mother would set fire to my face and beat it out with a brick."

She giggled. It was an odd thing to see in her.

I smiled. "You going to just sit there gawping at me, or are you going to pour me a drink?"

"Coffee laced with whiskey is what you need."

"Sounds about right."

She got up and went to the kitchen.

"You know, I keep going over it again and again in my mind. We had him. He was going to pay, God knows how much, millions. I had him hooked, and he had no way out but to pay and sign that damned confession. She and Tammy were home and dry.

And she just reaches over, picks up the gun, and blows Ronaldo away. Why would she do that, Dehan?"

She was quiet, making the coffee. When it started gurgling, she sighed and looked at me. "I forget who said it, but there is a quote by some wiseass about how if you want to know a person's intentions, you should ignore their words and look at their actions. So from that perspective, there is only one answer to your question. She would do that because she wanted them dead."

I sat, turning what she'd just said over in my head. It was so clear.

"That's right. That is absolutely right. She wanted dos Santos dead. That was exactly what she wanted."

She looked at me curiously. "Is that surprising?"

"Not really. But it's like one of those pictures where it looks like a scowling old man, and when you just change your perspective, suddenly it looks like a beautiful young woman. Suddenly, I see the other picture, and it all makes sense."

"Glad I could help."

"We have a long day ahead of us, Dehan. Let's get some bacon and mushrooms going, and a couple of eggs. I have a lot to explain to you, and then we need to make a plan."

So she gave us two more spiked coffees and started frying, while I started explaining.

EMMA'S CALL came at half eight. She was hysterical, sobbing and almost incoherent.

"John, thank God! I didn't know if you'd found your phone. I am going to pieces, John. What am I going to do. *I killed a man! John, do you understand? I shot and killed him!*"

"Take it easy."

"What are you talking about, take it easy? They'll send me to prison for life! You have to do something!"

"I said take it easy."

"What am I going to do? I can't go to prison, John. I can't! Do you know what they will do to a woman like me in prison?"

"Emma. Shut up."

I heard her swallow.

"In the first place, it was self-defense . . ."

"Self-defense . . . ?"

"That's right. There was you and me and Geronimo. If it ever comes to trial, you and me are telling the same story. He came at you with the gun. You struggled and somehow turned the gun on him."

"Yes, I see . . ."

"But it is never going to come to that, because I am the investigating officer, and I am going to pin the whole thing on dos Santos."

"You are?"

"You bet."

"Oh, John, how can I ever thank you? All I want is to get away and put this whole nightmare behind me."

"I know, baby. It's almost over."

"What about you?"

"Before you do your disappearing act, we need to talk about the box."

"Keep it. I'll put you in touch with a discreet buyer. You can open an account in Belize and have the money paid in there. Then you can live like a king for the rest of your life."

"When can I see you?"

"May I come over this afternoon? I'd like to collect Tammy's birthday present and say . . . not au revoir, but olive oil. I hope, when this is over . . ."

"Don't say it, Emma. If it's real, we'll do it."

"Yes. Yes, you're right."

"I'll see you at four. Will you bring Tammy? I've heard so much about her, I'd like to meet her at least once before you do your vanishing act."

"Of course. We'll be there at four."

I hung up and sat looking at Dehan. She stared back at me. After a moment I said, "Come on, let's go and see Geronimo."

We got to the Plaza at shortly after nine thirty. My car was still there, so Dehan dropped me off and headed back to the station to talk to the captain, who was in the midst of an acute anxiety attack. I checked at the desk and Geronimo dos Santos was still in the Royal Suite. I took the elevator and made my way up.

This time, he opened the door himself. He stood staring at me for a long moment, then turned and walked back toward the drawing room. I stepped in and closed the door behind me. I found him in a large armchair sulking among his chins. On the coffee table in front of him, he had a bottle of vodka and an empty shot glass.

"You planning on stopping anytime soon, Geronimo?"

He glowered at me sullenly.

"What?"

"Acting like an asshole. How many people do you plan to get killed before you stop? Is this how you do God's work, dos Santos? By going around getting people killed? Because let me tell you something, I am going to make it my business to ensure that the next person who gets killed is you." I stuck out my finger and pointed at him. "You are alive this morning because I jumped on Emma when she was going to pop you. You owe me your life."

His expression changed to one of calculating cunning. It was an effort to control the urge to smack him.

"We are alone right now, dos Santos. You know? I ought to give you a taste of what you gave me last night."

He swallowed and looked sick.

"You forced me."

"Bullshit!"

"You and Emma . . . I can't trust either of you . . ."

"*Bullshit!*"

He swallowed again. He looked scared.

"Between the two of you, you have fucked up a sweet deal— for no good reason! You because of your stupid obsession with

Tamara, and her because she wanted to play it smart. If you had both listened to me, you would have your precious goddamn box by now, and she would have her money and her damned sister." I approached the table and sat opposite him. "Now I am going to ask you one more time. Are you planning to stop?"

"What are you proposing?"

I'd been in the room thirty seconds and he was already making me mad.

"Maybe I didn't make myself clear. Next time you try to screw me over, I am going to blow that sick little head of yours clean of your multiple chins. Now I am going to ask you one. Last. Time. And if I don't get a clear answer, first, I am going to go over there and beat you to a sobbing pulp. Then, I am going to walk out of here and sell that box on the open market. *Then* I am going to put out a contract on you. So, Geronimo, are you ready to quit?"

He closed his eyes and seemed to shudder all over. Maybe it was the effort of having to make a commitment to not being stupid.

"Yes."

"We get one last shot at this. We do it my way and everybody wins. You step out of line by one inch, and I will kill you, personally."

"You have made yourself very clear."

"You do not get Tamara."

He opened his eyes and glared at me. His fat, white cheeks flushed red. I reached under my arm, pulled out my revolver, and cocked it. I took aim at his head. I am not honestly sure if I was planning to shoot him or not. His eyes bulged and all the pinkness drained from his face.

"All right! All right!"

"*Forget Tamara!*"

He nodded.

For good measure, I added, "It is the only way you get to stay alive." He nodded again.

I put my piece back under my arm and continued.

"I want ten million bucks, in a numbered account in Belize. Make no mistake, dos Santos. I know I can get a lot more. But I want this over with. Start pushing, try to get smart, and this deal disappears off the table faster than you can say, 'Please don't shoot.'"

"I can do that, no problem."

I threw my card on the table. He picked it up and looked at it. I pulled out my pen like I wanted to add something and gestured for him to give it back to me. He handed it over. I took an evidence bag from my pocket and slipped the card in.

"I take it your prints are not in the system."

He went crimson to the top of his scalp. "You are bluffing. You can't take prints from paper . . ."

"On the contrary. They are one of the best surfaces for taking prints. Though banisters, cell phones, guns, garden chairs, and tables are all pretty good too. Your prints are all over Emma's beach house, Geronimo, and all over my phone and my other gun. And even as we speak, there is a CSI team going over that house with a fine-tooth comb." I held up the card. "This is insurance. I am as implicated as you are. If you go down, the best I can hope for is to make a deal, but I go down too. However, my friend, if I go down, there are no deals for you. You go away for life." I stood. "Do yourself a favor. Be at my house today at three. I want to see my money in the account, then you get your box. And then you get the hell out of my city. I will make arrangements. Anything happens to Emma or Tammy, or me, you go down."

He sneered. "A regular Galahad."

"Don't bank on that, dos Santos. I'm an ugly son of a bitch. You don't want to see the dark side."

I left, wondering how much of what I had said was truth, and how much was an act.

TWENTY-FIVE

I STEPPED OUT INTO THE GLARE AND THE HEAT AND made my way to my car. I sat for ten minutes staring at nothing, seeing only my thoughts. I replayed for the thousandth time the scene from last night. Emma, exquisite, sobbing, pleading for my life. Dos Santos, grotesque, sneering, talking about using pliers to remove my fingers. Ronaldo, his mindless face vaguely surprised as he looked at the gun. And then all hell breaking loose. I saw her scrambling to her feet, racing frantically after him, her legs straddled in the doorway, taking aim.

I fired up the Jag and headed back to the station.

I DROPPED into my chair and stared at Dehan, who was staring back at me across the desk. She was good to stare at right then. "You have humanity, haven't you, Dehan?"

She raised an eyebrow. "I try to avoid it, but it's there. What can you do?"

"Did you talk to the captain?"

"He wants to see you. He wants to see us both."

"When?"

"As soon as you come in."

I looked at my watch. "That would be in about five minutes."

"You want a coffee?"

"More than anything in the world, apart from sleep."

She went away to get me some coffee. She had humanity.

Ten minutes later, we sat in front of the captain. He was looking at my face and seemed distressed.

"You look like hell, Stone."

"Yeah, I didn't have time to put my makeup on this morning."

"This is no joking matter."

"No, sir."

"I understand you and Detective Dehan have your own methods, but I can't help feeling this thing has got a little out of hand."

"I have to take full responsibility for that, sir. I did not anticipate that dos Santos would drug me and kidnap me. I had never encountered that before."

His frown deepened. "It's like something out of a Sam Spade novel."

Dehan coughed. "Dashiell Hammett, sir. Sam Spade was the character . . . sir . . ."

"Thank you, Detective Dehan. I'll try to remember that." His voice could have etched metal. He looked back at me. "I don't know what to say, John. Have you got a grip on this case? Do you need time to convalesce?"

"No, sir. I am confident I can wrap it up today."

He looked surprised. "Today?"

"Yes, sir. Detective Dehan and I discussed it at length this morning, and I have made most of the arrangements."

He nodded and looked at Dehan. "You feel equally confident, Dehan?"

"Yes, sir."

"You need backup?"

"Just one unmarked car, Captain, outside my house. I'd like to explain my plan . . ."

He sat back and gave a smile that hovered between admiration and irony. It is not an easy smile to pull off.

AT TWO FIFTY, I was ready in my house. I felt like I needed to lie down and die for a week, preferably on a beach in the Caribbean. I took a fortifying slug of Irish and sat down to wait. I had set myself up in my armchair, with a coffee table in front of me. I had my laptop on the breakfast bar playing Mozart softly in the background. I was ready.

The doorbell rang at three on the dot. I let him ring three times before I opened. He had an attaché case with him.

"You said at three. I am not accustomed to being kept waiting."

"Then get accustomed. Sit down."

He glanced at me resentfully, like I was being unkind, and sat on the sofa. Then he offered me an ingratiating smile. "Mozart. The number one Flute Concerto. G Major."

I offered him a sour look back. "It eases me. I need easing." I sat.

"Well, Stone—John, if I may—shall we get down to business? You have the box?"

"What's your hurry?"

"My hurry? There is surely no need to prolong things. In view of what has happened, I am naturally eager to leave the country . . ."

I smiled. "I bet you are. Just answer me a few questions."

He sighed. "Is this necessary? I have not time to waste."

"It's necessary. There are things I don't understand. Last night you were going to take my fingers off with a pair of pliers. Today you can indulge me. Have a drink with me and answer my questions. Alternatively, you can get the fuck out of my house."

I put the bottle and a glass on the table. He looked at it with distaste.

"Whiskey . . ."

"I have no vodka. Drink."

He poured himself a shot, sipped, winced, and put the glass down.

"You work for the Vatican."

"In a manner of speaking."

"In what manner of speaking?"

He shifted his ass and looked uncomfortable. "It is a semiofficial office, based near Santiago de Compostela, in Spain, in the castle of Soto Maior. I am the personal assistant of Cardinal Guzman, and our mission is to acquire unique treasures for the Holy Mother Church."

"At whatever cost . . . to the people letting those treasures go."

He made a "who gives a shit?" face and said, "When an item belongs properly to the Church, I feel any means are justified."

It wasn't the first time he'd said that, and I thought about it for a moment.

"So Hugh Duffy had this . . . box. And in your opinion, it belonged properly to the Church. So you set about looking for a sexy young woman . . ."

He expostulated, "Please! Give me credit for being a little more subtle than a mule!"

"Of course. You did your homework, you found out about his fiancée . . ."

"And I set about seeking *the perfect* actress to play the part of his fiancée." He looked pleased with himself. "And I have to say, she was brilliant. Quite captivating. She could have been a star, Detective. She had a quality about her that just made you love her."

"So that's what you hired her for. To make Duffy fall in love with her."

"And when she had won his trust, then to take the box."

"Did she know what was in the box?"

The complacent smile slipped from his face. "Not to begin with, but that fool Duffy told her what it was."

I snarled, "Isn't that what you wanted, for him to trust her? And once she knew what it was, she realized you were paying her a fraction of a fraction of what it was worth. She realized she could get several thousand times what you were paying her on a specialized market."

He studied my face a moment. "So, I have answered your questions. Shall we do business?"

I nodded, reached in my pocket, and tossed him over a sheet of paper with the details of a numbered account Dehan and I had opened that morning in Belize. On a sudden impulse, I said, "But the price went up."

He glared at me, then surprised me by asking, "How much?" As I had suspected, I was still well within his budget.

"Fifteen."

He wrenched open his attaché case, and I saw it had a laptop built into it. He tapped furiously while muttering, "Do not push me too far, Stone. This far and no further." He turned the computer toward me, like he was trying to wrench it off his lap, and showed me the screen. There were fifteen million dollars poised to be transferred into my account. "Now," he said, "show me the box."

I smiled at him. "I wonder just how far I could push you."

"No further!"

I reached down beside my chair and pulled up the wooden box that Emma had given me. I placed it on the table.

He narrowed his eyes at it. "Let me see. I don't trust you." Then he shifted his gaze to me. "You haven't looked inside? I find that hard to believe . . ."

I shrugged. "What difference does it make? I am not an expert. As far as I know, it could be anything. I've got my money. That's all I care about. At a cool fifteen percent, I am in clover, dos Santos."

"Let me see it," he grunted.

"What is that, two and a quarter million a year? I figure I could be happy living on that."

I was playing for time, and he was beginning to sense it. He sat forward. "Why won't you let me see it?"

"I am not stopping you, dos Santos. I am just wondering if you really do want to see what's in this box."

His face flushed. "Of course I do! Stop playing games, Stone! I am warning you! I have not transferred the money yet!"

"I am aware of that. But you will, don't worry. Wait, I think I hear somebody coming . . ."

He turned and stared at the door. There were footsteps approaching from the sidewalk; they sounded like a woman's high heels. They climbed the steps to the door, and the doorbell rang. He turned back and glared at me.

"What is this, Stone? You are going too far! I am warning you!"

I smiled, picked up the box, and rose to open the door.

TWENTY-SIX

She stepped through the doorway and immediately put her arms around my neck and kissed me. Maybe she sensed I was not really responsive. She pulled back and held my face in her hands, frowning, examining the swelling and the bruising.

"Oh, you poor darling. What did they do to you?"

"I'll survive, which is more than can be said for Ronaldo."

She frowned. "Are you very cross with me?" As she spoke, she noticed the box in my hand. "What are you doing?"

I smiled. "Come on in." I closed the door behind her and said, "Take a seat, Emma. We have some things to discuss."

As I said it, dos Santos stood up. He had a face that would have made a Carolina reaper wince. When he spoke, his voice was a rasp. "This is intolerable, Stone. My patience is not limitless."

"Neither is mine, dos Santos. Shut up and sit down. We have business to transact. You don't get the box and I don't get the money until Emma and Tammy are safe."

Emma stared at dos Santos, then at me, and made several false starts in trying to say something. "John, you should have . . . This is not . . . What are you . . . ?"

"Sit down, Emma. Have a drink."

I sat her in the chair opposite mine, put a glass in front of her, and nudged the whiskey bottle her way. "Help yourself."

I sat and looked at them both, one after the other and back again.

"Where were we, Geronimo? Oh yes." I turned to Emma. "Geronimo is about to transfer fifteen million bucks into a numbered account for me. Naturally, as you are my partner in crime, Emma, part of that money should go to you. Also quite naturally, Geronimo was saying that, before he makes the transfer, he wants to see the box and its contents for himself."

She was shaking her head as I was speaking. "John, really, I want no part of this. I am not cut out for this kind of thing. I am not a criminal . . ."

"You saying I am?"

"You know what I mean."

"You going to say no to half of fifteen million bucks, Emma? Seven and a half million is nothing to be sneezed at."

"Please, John, this is not what we agreed. Just give me Tammy's birthday present and let me go."

I snapped my fingers. "You know what it is, dos Santos. Emma is English. Seven and a half million bucks, in pounds sterling, is chicken feed. I'll tell you what we'll do—you make that fifteen million pounds sterling, and then I think Emma will be happy, and I can let you see the box."

He was shaking visibly. "I swear to God, Stone . . ."

"Do it."

He tapped at his keyboard, then savagely turned it for me to look at. Over twenty million dollars. And he still hadn't reached his limit. I smiled at Emma. Her hands were trembling.

"John, I am very frightened, and I would like to go now."

"We are almost done, Emma. I am just trying to ensure your safety in the future. You understand that, don't you?"

"Yes, and I am very grateful."

"Stone! *Let me see the box!*"

"In just a moment, dos Santos. I just have a couple of questions I need to ask Emma."

Her eyes fixed on me. "Questions?"

I laughed. "All these years as a cop, it's become a habit. I have to understand *how* things happened the way they did. You know what I mean? Like last night, when you just reached over, cool as a cucumber, picked up Ronaldo's gun, and boom! And then you were about to pop Geronimo here too. See? I don't understand that. I don't understand what made you do that."

"I panicked."

"You panicked? I can understand you panicking when he's holding the gun. But after he laid it on the table, and I finally had these fucking idiots talking, *then* you panicked? *Then* you pick up the gun, and with no provocation at all, you kill him?"

She stared hard at her hands in her lap. "Yes."

I blew out through my teeth. Dos Santos was watching me like a hawk. I said, "I have to tell you, Emma, you panic with a hell of a lot of cool. Because you were as cold as ice. And when you went through that door after dos Santos, and you stopped and adopted that stance, you looked just like a pro. You sure you're not CIA undercover?"

"Don't be ridiculous."

"So explain it. How come you were so cold? How come the professional shooting stance?"

"Training."

"*Training?* What kind of training?"

"When I moved to the States and Tammy explained to me the kind of trouble she was in, I took several firearms courses, to advanced degree. I suppose it kicked in last night."

"Huh. That's a good answer."

"It happens to be the truth."

"I believe you."

"Can I go now?"

"Yes, Stone, enough of this stupid inquisition. Let us finalize the deal and be done with it."

"I am almost done, dos Santos. Let's see a little of that Christian patience."

"It *is* becoming tiresome, John."

"I know. Just bear with me. I am just curious about Tammy."

She sighed.

"What about her? It's a shame you didn't bring her. She could have answered these questions herself. You know, she and Duffy got real close. He was, and still is, crazy about her. What I have never understood, from the very beginning, is why she left him? At first I thought she was in love with that loser Steve. But it turns out she hated him enough to shoot him in the heart. So if she was after the kind of money this . . ." I lifted up the box and waved it at her. ". . . this box could bring her, why didn't she just stay with Duffy?"

"I suppose she just didn't love him."

"Nah." I shook my head. "Shall I tell you what I think?"

"I suppose we can't stop you."

"I think she had every intention of going back to Duffy. She is too smart a cookie to pass up a chance like that. But after losing her parents, twice, and her sister, she was not about to start trusting anyone, ever again. What she needed, what she was hungry for, was a fortune of her own. Money in the bank, that is something you can trust. And the only reason she went to see Steve was to have him fence the goods. He was the only connection she had with the criminal underworld. She went to him to help her find a buyer. It was a stupid thing to do."

Dos Santos was sweating. "An interesting theory. Now, can we *please* get on . . ."

I sighed. "I guess you were having her tailed, right? It's the obvious thing to do. And when she took off to the Big Apple, you came after her. You hired Danny to get a couple of heavies together and go and pay her and Steve a visit. Danny picked the Sanchez brothers, and they dropped in on Steve while Tammy was there. This is pure deduction, but I'm pretty sure it's as near as dammit to what happened." I watched Emma's face as I spoke.

"They're laying into Steve, asking him where the box is. Tammy is begging them to leave him alone, but she can see that even the promise of all that cash is not enough to keep his mouth shut. He is going to spill. Especially when they start talking about mutilation and killing. So she makes a play. She pretends she is going for the box, but what she pulls out of the drawer is a .38 revolver that she has persuaded her husband to bring to her from San Francisco."

Emma was staring at her hands. She didn't say anything. Dos Santos looked like a man trying to crush a wasp between his buttocks. He suddenly erupted. "Yes! You are correct in every particular as far as I am concerned. You are a clever man. Unfortunately, Tammy is not here to confirm her part. Now! At last! Are we *done*?"

"Almost. Tammy knows that Steve is no longer any damn use to her, plus there is the risk that he is going to talk. So she blows him away. She knows that Danny and the Sanchez boys are going to be in shock for a couple of seconds. Nobody expected cute little Tammy to pull a gun, much less be able to use it. So she blows a hole in Ernesto too. Danny panics and runs. Now she has a choice: kill Alfonso or go after Danny. She goes after Danny because he is going to report back to you, dos Santos. Trouble is, she loses him in the night, and meantime, Alfonso helps Ernesto to get away, leaving the crime scene that would later go cold. Ernesto died and wound up in the river. Which left Danny. And here is where it gets a bit weird."

Her voice was wooden. "Weird how?"

"Weird because Danny got murdered just a few months later, by a very elegant, beautiful woman with short black hair and green eyes and a deep Southern drawl. She picked him up in a bar and left with him and then shot him."

Geronimo was frowning.

Emma shrugged. "He was mugged by a hooker."

"No, that won't wash. I told you that Tammy made a few mistakes, and this was one of them. I guess she was desperate. But she made the mistake of shooting him with the same gun she used to kill Steve."

She looked at me like I was crazy. "You just said she was a sophisticated woman with a Southern drawl, black hair, and green eyes. I can't imagine a woman less like Tamara. Really, John, this has gone on too long. For goodness' sake, let's end it! Keep the bloody money! I don't want it! Just let me get back to Tammy and start over!"

"Relax. That is exactly what I intend to do."

And then there was a ring at the door.

TWENTY-SEVEN

Dos Santos stood. He was trembling. "*What now?*"

Emma looked really scared. I picked up the box again. "Come on, have you lost all your faith in human greed? It's nothing."

I stood, crossed the room, and stood with my hand on the door handle. "You see, I kept turning it over, again and again, and whichever way I looked at it, it just didn't make sense." I opened the door and smiled. "Hi, just hold on one second, would you?" I walked back a couple of steps so that I could look at dos Santos and Emma where they were sitting, watching me anxiously. "And then one evening, it hit me. It was obvious. I did my research on Google, and there it was." I turned back to the door and said, "Come on in. Join the party."

Dos Santos jumped to his feet. Emma went white. Hugh Duffy saw dos Santos first and smiled at him amiably. "Why, hello! I didn't expect to see you here. It's been a long time . . ." He advanced toward him with his hand held out, and as he did so, he caught sight of Emma. He started saying, "Oh, forgive me . . ." then stopped and did a kind of double take. Her expression was one of absolute horror. He faltered, stared at me, and then back at Emma. "Tammy?"

She shook her head furiously. "No!"

Dos Santos' jaw dropped. "*What?*"

I picked up a glass and poured a generous measure of whiskey into it. I handed it to Duffy. "Sit down, Mr. Duffy, and have a drink. You are going to need one."

He stared at me and then at the glass, like he didn't understand what either of us were doing in his life. Then he sat. I put the glass in front of him. He ignored it and shook his head at Emma.

"Your hair . . . you look so different. What happened? Why . . . I don't understand."

I sat again and put the box on the table in front of me. "It is a rare gift that some actors have. Boris Karloff had it; Meryl Streep is another. It's a kind of chameleon effect, where they take on a role to such an extent that they actually become a different person. The change inside is so profound that they actually appear to change physically. But with Tammy, I think it went deeper even than that, didn't it, Emma? Because I don't think even the Tammy you met, dos Santos, was the real Tammy. I don't think there ever was a real Tammy. I think there was just a hollow shell, searching for an identity, sustained by an unquestionable talent for drama.

"The first thing that struck me about your house, when I went there, was that there was absolutely no identity in it. Just the picture of your parents, the books by Stanislavski, and a couple of self-help books. Not a single thing to show who Tamara was. Only the scrapbook."

"I am not Tammy. I am Emma."

Duffy stared at me. "What is going on, Stone. Who is Emma?"

"Emma? Emma was Tammy's sister. She died when Tammy was five. But recently, I suspect Tammy has revived her, to keep herself safe in a world where everybody she loves gets snatched away from her. In the end, she came to rely so much on Emma's strength that she became Emma completely, and

Tammy, in fear for her life, hid away inside, where nobody could find her."

Emma curled up in her chair and began to sob. Dos Santos still looked like he'd seen his own ghost. "How did I not see?"

"It struck me yesterday, when you said you had only seen Tammy very briefly. Even then, I figure you were focusing more on what Hugh Duffy was going to be seeing than on what you were actually seeing at the time. With two years in between, some skillful makeup, and Tammy's talent, I thought it was possible she could pull the wool over your eyes. Even so, she took the precaution of seeing you out on the terrace, by moonlight. It also made sense of why she was more keen to kill you than to get your money. When we had you nailed down and ready to deal, instead of closing, she went and blew the whole thing by trying to kill you. It made sense when I realized, if you had recognized her at any point, she would be screwed three ways to Sunday.

"The same applied to Baxter, didn't it, Emma? Somehow he had tracked you down and worked it out. The day I met you, he had just been in to let you know, and start putting the squeeze on you before handing you over to dos Santos. That afternoon I followed you to Baxter's office. I didn't realize it at the time, but while I was waiting downstairs, you were up there shooting him through the heart. That's your favorite shot, right? That's how you feel—why shouldn't they?" I shook my head and gave a mirthless laugh. "Once it dawned on me, it all made sense. The way everybody described Tammy was a perfect description of Emma. Looking at Tammy's photograph, Emma looked exactly like her older sister. Only it was actually her."

I turned back to dos Santos. "She needed you dead. With you and Baxter out of the way, she would be free to exploit her expert husband and sell . . . the box."

"Husband?" It was Duffy. He was staring at her. She was still curled up, sobbing into her hands.

"I'm sorry to be brutal, Mr. Duffy, but she has two of them. One back in San Francisco, the other in Manhattan."

He shook his head, bewildered. "*Why?*"

I nodded. "That is not so easy to explain, Mr. Duffy. But let's start by acceding at last to Mr. dos Santos' repeated request."

Emma looked up. Her face was drenched, but she was one of those very rare women who do not go puffy and red when they cry. She looked even more beautiful. I pushed the box across the table toward dos Santos. His eyes were bulging, and his hands were trembling.

Emma was shaking her head. "Stone, no . . ."

I glanced at her. Her cut-glass English was gone.

There was a shriek from dos Santos. He was on his feet. "*What is this? What is this shit? What are you trying to pull, Stone?*"

I smiled at him, then at Emma. "Isn't that what this whole thing has been about? The da Vinci portrait of Clarice Orsini? The brand-new wife of Lorenzo de' Medici?"

Dos Santos screamed. "*What? This?*" He held up the painting, smashed it on the floor, and stamped on it. His face was red, and I could see veins standing out on his head and his neck as he slammed his heel down again and again. "*This piece of second-rate shit? This piece of fucking shit?*"

He stopped, panting, and glared at Emma. "Where is it?"

I reached down beside my chair and pulled up Tammy's birthday present. "I happen to know that Tamara Gunthersen was born Tamara Hunter, in West Sussex, England, on March 16, 1995. So this was never going to be her birthday present. Also, you *are* Tamara Gunthersen, so there is that too. So if this is not her birthday present, what is it?"

I turned to Duffy. "I take it you are not familiar with that picture, Mr. Duffy, and that it never went missing from your collection."

He shook his head. "It is a very second-rate imitation. I have never seen it before."

"How about this?"

I pulled on the bow and peeled back the paper to reveal a very exquisite wooden box of what seemed to be Byzantine design. Duffy was frowning at it with curiosity. Dos Santos was trembling and sweating, and Emma's face was creasing up. "John, please . . ."

I opened it up. It contained a small, beautifully illuminated Bible and a cup ground out of polished stone.

Duffy nodded. "Yes, that's mine. It is the Thomas de Ahisi Bible. It is priceless. And the cup . . ."

Dos Santos cut across him. His voice was like the voice of a snake. "It is not yours. It belongs to the Holy Mother. You are not even a Catholic; you are an unholy Protestant. That treasure belongs by right to the Holy Roman Church. It is the sacred Holy Grail in which our Lord Jesus Christ converted water into wine, his holy blood."

I raised an eyebrow at him. "This is the Holy Grail? How can you possibly know that? There must be thousands of stone cups like this. You can't even carbon-date it."

"It has provenance."

"It has *provenance*?"

Duffy, who was still staring at Emma, nodded and glanced at me. "It's true. It has an unbroken line of documents going all the way back to St. Peter. He took it to Rome and handed it over, upon his death, to the leader of the Christian Church who took over from him. Thus it was handed down to successive church leaders until it was given to the Emperor Constantine."

Dos Santos took over. "When Constantinople was overrun by the infidels, the cup was rescued by a Spanish knight, Don Rafael de Aragon, Marques de Soto Maior. It was preserved at his castle in Galicia until the eighteenth century, when it was stolen by the then marques' youngest son, who took it to Mexico, possibly planning to sell it. As an act of penitence, the Marques de Soto Maior devoted his life, his wealth, and his castle to the purpose of accumulating sacred treasures for the Holy Mother Church. There is a cardinal always in residence overseeing the treasures. And it has been my life's work to track down and reacquire the Grail."

Duffy looked at him curiously, then turned to me. "It was not until 1856 that my great-great-grandfather won it in a poker game from that thief's grandson. I have examined the provenance and had it looked at by experts. It is almost certainly real." He turned back to dos Santos. "And I am sorry, Mr. dos Santos, but it is not for sale."

I laughed. "Oh, Mr. dos Santos does not intend to buy it from you, Mr. Duffy." I reached out and pulled the box back. "He employed Tamara Gunthersen to show up at your house and seduce you so that she could steal this treasure and hand it over to dos Santos. But she got other ideas and thought she'd take it for herself instead and sell it on the open market."

Dos Santos gave one of his hysterical screams. "*Enough! I can't take it anymore! Enough talk! Talk! Talk! You have what you wanted! You have asked your fucking questions! Now give me the box!*"

I pointed at the laptop. "Press the button and show me the transaction has gone through. Then you get the box."

His eyes were wide. He hesitated a fraction of a second, then hit the Enter key and spun the computer so that I could see. I had just become a multimillionaire. I smiled at him and then at Emma.

"Geronimo dos Santos, Tamara Gunthersen, I am placing you both under arrest on multiple charges of murder, attempted murder, conspiracy to murder, and theft. You do not have to say anything, but anything you do say may be taken down and used against you in a court of law."

And then all hell broke loose.

TWENTY-EIGHT

DOS SANTOS SLAMMED THE CASE SHUT, STOOD, AND swung it violently at my head. I put up my arms to protect myself, and the case struck my shoulder. Emma—Tamara—let out a piercing scream and leapt at dos Santos as he grabbed for the box on the table, scratching at his flabby face with her nails.

I got to my feet shouting, "*Sit down! Both of you!*" But dos Santos put all his four hundred plus pounds into a huge back-hander that sent Tammy sprawling across the room. I reached for him, yelling, "*Give me some backup here!*" Outside, car doors slammed and feet pounded the blacktop. Dos Santos heard them too, and despair, added to his massive weight, made him a formidable opponent. He put his hand on my face and heaved. I crashed back into my chair. Next thing, he was reaching under his jacket, and he had a sleek, black Sig Sauer P226 in his hand, waving it around like an aerosol.

I shouted, "*Stand down! He's armed!*"

He glared at me and hissed like a fat snake. "Mozart! You were recording the whole thing! I should shoot you dead right here and now. Tell them to withdraw, or the first to die will be your precious billionaire. Next will be Tammy, and after that, you. *Do it!*"

"Pull back, Dehan. You know what to do."

He put the box in the hip pocket of his jacket and waved the gun at Duffy. "Up, you. Come on! Up!" Duffy got uncertainly to his feet. "Open the door and step out. Remember, I have you covered at every step."

He grabbed him by the scruff of the neck and shoved him toward the door. Duffy opened it and dos Santos hustled up close to him, with the Sig shoved into his lower back. They stepped outside and moved slowly down the steps. I stood in the doorway.

"Dehan, I want a unit following dos Santos. As soon as he is clear, you need to get in here and take Tammy into custody."

As I said it, I heard a scream like a banshee with a hornet in her ass, and a freight train slammed into me from behind and sent me crashing down the stairs. I sprawled on my face and saw Tammy's feet pounding the path toward my gate. I had a piercing pain in my head, but I scrambled to my feet and staggered after her. That was when I saw she had my kitchen knife in her hand and was racing like a thing possessed toward dos Santos, who was standing by a silver Aston Martin Vanquish. I shouted without thinking.

"*Tammy! No!*"

Dos Santos turned, grabbed Duffy, and hurled him at Tammy. Duffy stumbled, reached for Tammy's shoulders, and gripped her, searching her face. "Tammy, sweetheart, listen to me. Leave it— this is not for you. Let him keep it. We can fix this. I have connections . . ."

She was doing a kind of dance, trying to get around him, trying to get past him at dos Santos, who was wrenching open the door of his Vanquish. Suddenly she was screaming, "*Get out of my way!*" She lunged, he grappled with her, and the knife flashed, once, twice, three times, and Duffy was sinking to his knees.

I was halfway across the road and turned back, racing for my Jag, bellowing, "*Move in! Move in! Get a paramedic here now! Call an ambulance! Man down! Man down!*"

I heard the Vanquish's tires scream, and as I clambered into the Jag, I saw Tammy jumping over the door of her open-top Mercedes. I heard the sirens wailing behind me and took off after dos Santos. He screeched into Neill Avenue as I accelerated after him. A vintage Jag, however cool, is no match for a modern Aston Martin supercar. As long as we stayed in the city, I had a chance of staying with him, but once he hit the freeway, I didn't have a hope in hell. I radioed in.

"In pursuit of a silver Aston Martin Vanquish headed east on Neill Avenue toward Benjamin Nolan. Request a chopper."

By the time I had finished, he was already jumping the lights at the junction and thundering north on Nolan. I followed to the tune of honking horns and squealing brakes. I knew what was coming next.

"He's headed for the junction with the Bronx Pelham Parkway." That would lead him to the New England Thruway. If he did that, I would lose him. "Have you got me that damned chopper?"

"Working on it, Detective."

Ahead, I saw him hit the Parkway and take the corner at sixty miles an hour. The car cornered flat and stuck to the road like it was nailed to it. The massive V12 on a Vanquish will hurl it from zero to sixty in just over three seconds. I took the corner and floored the pedal, but the Aston Martin was moving away from me like I was stationary. In a few seconds, he was going to hit spaghetti junction. If he took the I-95, he would vanish in seconds.

"Dispatch! Where is that damned chopper?"

I hit a hundred and ten miles per hour as I crossed the bridge. Ahead, he must have been doing a hundred and fifty, because he was pulling away from me at forty miles per hour at least. But he didn't take the I-95 turnoff. He rocketed under the New England Thruway and kept going, east and north. And suddenly, I knew where he was going.

I'd been checking my rearview, and now I saw Tamara's Mercedes closing in on me.

"Dispatch, request immediate backup, headed north on Pelham Bridge Road. Suspect headed for the islands at New Rochelle."

"Copy that."

Tamara passed me doing a hundred and thirty. I was creeping up to one twenty, but I didn't think the old Jag could give me much more.

We had to slow as we hit Shore Road and the sleepy suburbs that surround it. Soon, I was cruising through the town with Tammy a few yards ahead of me. I was scanning left and right. I knew he was here. I could feel him.

Then I saw the Vanquish. He'd dumped it in the marina parking lot. Ahead of me, Tamara had seen it too and was dithering. I dropped into second, gunned the engine, and thundered past her on her right. Then I spun the wheel and turned down Town Dock Road onto the docks, with Tamara screaming on my heels.

He was there, on the jetty, clambering into a small speedboat. I screeched to a halt by the steps that led down to the quay and jumped out. I heard the Mercedes skid to a stop behind me. Then Tamara's voice:

"Freeze!"

I turned just in time to get pistol-whipped across my head. My head was having a bad couple of days. I sank to my knees. Through a haze of pain, I saw Tamara running down toward dos Santos' launch. I heard shouts and feet running and turned to see a group of men coming toward me. I pulled myself to my feet and held up my badge. "NYPD. I need a launch! *Now!*"

A big guy with an Italian face frowned at me. "I got one. You okay, pal?"

I pointed at dos Santos. "Follow that speedboat . . ."

"Seriously?"

"Yes!"

"Okay! I'm Tony."

Down on the jetty, things were not going as dos Santos had planned. He was pulling out of the harbor and moving off at speed, but Tammy was standing behind him, holding a gun to his head.

We clambered into Tony's speedboat and took off after them. They turned into the Glen Island strait and accelerated toward Huckleberry Island. They were maybe a hundred yards ahead of us, slapping across the water and raising great plumes of spray as they went, holding their position. We were not gaining on them. I turned to Tony.

"What the hell is on that island?"

He looked bemused. The wind whipped his words away as he spoke. "Nothing. It's deserted."

Now they were banking, looping into a long curve around the northern tip of the small landmass. Whatever they were after was clearly on the other side.

"There is a natural bay around there," he shouted. "Maybe they have a yacht."

"Can't you go any faster?"

"She's at top speed!"

As we came around the headland after them, I saw what dos Santos had come for. It wasn't a yacht. There was a broad bay with a sandy beach, as Tony had said, and sitting in the bay, bobbing on the gentle waves, was a twelve-seater seaplane. Dos Santos was approaching it fast, and somebody on board was opening the door and firing up the rotors.

Tony grinned. "If I ram him, will the city buy me a new boat?"

"Don't put yourself at risk, Tony. We stand down. We let them get away."

"Are you kidding?"

He aimed the prow of the boat at the seaplane and accelerated to top speed. Dos Santos was pulling up by the near float. I was searching in my mind, trying to anticipate what the hell Tamara thought she was going to do. She heard us approaching and turned to look. She raised her gun to careful aim and fired. The shot went wide. Dos Santos was reaching up frantically for the door. I saw Tamara lean against him. She pressed the revolver against his back and fired. Suddenly she had her hands to her face, screaming. The gun went over the side, and she was on her knees, shaking dos Santos like she couldn't believe he was dead, making out we had shot him. Hands were reaching down for her from the plane.

I saw her hand slip in his pocket, and then she was clambering aboard and the plane was accelerating away down the river, rising, climbing into the air.

We pulled up beside dos Santos' launch, and I clambered aboard. He was slumped against the gunwale, bleeding profusely. I felt his pulse in his neck; it was just a flutter. I looked back toward the shore. I could see the red-and-blue flashing of police units. I looked over at Tony. "Radio in—we are going to need an ambulance."

Dos Santos' eyes seemed to clear for a moment, and he focused on my face. He was an ugly, pasty gray color. He was trying to talk, and I leaned close. "You," he hissed, "you will go to hell for this . . ."

The last words he ever heard were his own, telling himself he was going to hell. That's how I choose to see it anyhow.

I felt in his pocket, but the box was gone, as I knew it would be.

Tony threw me a line, and we tied dos Santos' boat to his, then towed it back to the harbor. Dehan was there with half a dozen cops waiting for us on the quay. She helped me up out of the launch, searching my very bruised and battered face.

"Are you okay?"

I shrugged. "She got away. I'm sorry."

"And dos Santos?"

"Dead."

She looked down at his body, where the cops were trying to lift him out.

"I guess he'll be facing trial somewhere else."

I snorted. "Yeah, maybe."

TWENTY-NINE

THE CAPTAIN DIDN'T LOOK PLEASED. WE SAT LOOKING at him across his desk, while he sat looking at the glaring sunshine outside.

"It's a less than satisfactory outcome, John. I'm not blaming you, but I have to say that it isn't up to your usual standard. Either of you."

"No, sir," I said. "We are not satisfied with the result either."

Dehan said, "Have you heard from the hospital, Captain?"

"Duffy is in a serious condition, but he will live. There is also news of the plane, which is why I asked you to come up here. They found the wreckage of the seaplane out at Montauk Point."

I frowned. "What about the bodies?"

"Two pilots. Tamara Gunthersen's body was probably washed out to sea."

"What does the ME say about cause of death?"

The captain looked surprised. "They crashed in a plane. What do you expect him to say?"

"Well, sir, I am guessing that dos Santos, with his resources, employed competent pilots. In this weather, there is little reason to crash. So I'm wondering why they did."

He looked impatient. "He has barely had time to look at

them, but there will be a full report on the cause of the crash and the cause of death. Let's not try to complicate it any further."

"Yes, sir."

He looked at us in turn and seemed to relent a little. "However," he said, "I must congratulate you both on resolving a very complex mystery, even if the body count was rather high."

Dehan spoke up. "Thank you, sir, but we did not in fact cause any of those deaths. Tamara Gunthersen turned out to be a pretty lethal woman. In my opinion, Detective Stone did well to come out of this alive."

The captain gazed at her through hooded eyes that were probably meant to be intimidating. She met them with a smile. Dehan is not easy to intimidate.

"As I said," he went on, "I must congratulate you. Your recording via the webcam on your laptop was very effective. You have quite a flair for the dramatic yourself, John. It is just a shame we won't get to prosecute anyone with the evidence you garnered."

Dehan was in a voluble mood and spoke up again, with a grin that bordered on the insolent. "Ms. Gunthersen has at least saved the city the cost of an expensive trial. Sir."

"That is not an appropriate observation, Detective Dehan."

"No, sir."

"All right. It has been a very trying case, for both of you, but especially you, John. I suggest you take a few days off to recuperate."

We thanked him and left. It was six o'clock. I dropped Dehan at her apartment on Simpson Street and made my way home. I had a shower, ate a steak, and by eight o'clock I was in bed with a book, falling asleep as the lines crossed in front of my eyes. Gradually, blissful unconsciousness enfolded me.

I LAY STARING at the darkened ceiling, wondering what had woken me up. I looked at my clock. It said 2:02. I was still tired.

My eyes were heavy. Then the doorbell gave a prolonged jangle, and I knew that was what had woken me. I wondered what the hell Dehan could want at that time of the morning and staggered down the stairs to open the front door. It wasn't Dehan.

It was Tamara. She stood looking up at me with that face that should have belonged to an angel. She looked scared and vulnerable.

"I couldn't do it." She said it like it should make sense to me.

I stepped aside. "Come in."

She stepped in and placed her hands on my bare chest. "John, I am so sorry. Tell me you'll forgive me. I was out of my mind. I was so scared of what that monster would do to me."

"You stabbed Hugh Duffy three times in the stomach."

"I was out of my mind. I know it was wrong. You have to believe me."

"I don't have to believe anything."

I walked away from her into the kitchen and started making coffee.

She followed, but stopped in the middle of the floor. She looked like a beautiful, frightened child. "You are right to be angry."

"Why did you kill the pilots?"

"They were flying to Bermuda. They were going to take the box to Spain. I had to come back. I had to come back to you."

"Why?"

She smiled. "Because we are partners, remember? We are going to sell the box together. You are going to fix all this. The way you fixed it before, for Emma."

I nodded. "Have you got the box?"

"Yes." She reached in her pocket and pulled it out to show me. "There is nobody left now to stop us. Baxter is dead, dos Santos is dead."

"A lot of people are dead, Tamara."

"But they are not important people. People die. People come and go. Emma taught me that. They are not important. Important people are Emma and me, and you can be important too, if you join us. Steve could have been important, but he was stupid."

I poured two cups of coffee and reached in the cupboard for the whiskey. I laced both cups and pushed one across the breakfast bar for her.

"And if I don't?"

She laughed. "Come on! Don't tease."

She came forward and picked up her cup. We were like two old friends having a chat. She sipped and smiled. "So what's the plan?"

"The plan is you hand yourself over to the cops."

She didn't seem to register. She blinked a couple of times. "What?"

"I said, the plan is, Tamara, you hand yourself over to the cops. It's over. You are done killing people. The box goes back to Duffy, and you go into psychiatric care. It's over."

She sighed. "Come on, John, cut it out. We sell the box, we go away, you and me and Emma."

I put down my cup and walked around the bar to stand in front of her. "Tamara Gunthersen, I am putting you under arrest for multiple homicides and attempted homicides . . ."

The scream seemed to tear the whole night in half. The blade flashed. I stepped back and stumbled, and that probably saved my life. I fell back on the floor, and she fell on top of me, plunging the blade down toward my throat. I gripped her wrist with both my hands, but I was holding up the full weight of her body and I could feel the steel tip inching closer, until the point was pricking my skin. She leaned forward, straddling my chest, and heaved.

And then the door busted open. I heard Dehan's voice shouting, and I have never been so happy to hear anything in my whole life. She bellowed, *"Drop the knife!"*

Instead, Tamara raised herself up for a lunge that I knew would skewer my neck to the floor. I heard her scream of rage a fraction of a second before I heard the crack of Dehan's .38, and

Tamara's beautiful, tragic body sank slowly to the floor by my side.

Dehan rushed to me, checked I was okay, and then checked Tamara. I sat up with my back against the wall.

"What . . . Why are you here?"

She spoke into her radio instead of answering. "Dispatch, this is Detective Dehan of the Forty-Third Precinct, requesting an ambulance at Haight Avenue. One female, seriously injured . . . Also any unit in the area to respond . . ."

And far off I heard the wail of approaching sirens.

EPILOGUE

THE AMBULANCE HAD GONE, WITH THE PATROL CAR. IT was three in the morning, and Dehan was in the kitchen making scrambled eggs on rye, and more coffee. I watched her awhile, feeling numb and in pain at the same time, and deeply confused also. I sat gingerly at the table and sipped my laced coffee.

"Dehan?"

"Yuh."

"Why are you here?"

"I came to save your butt, remember?"

"No. I mean yes, but no, that's not what I mean. I mean, why are you here saving my butt? How did you know?"

She sighed and shook her head, and spilled eggs onto the toasted rye on the plate. "Come and eat."

I made my way around to the kitchen table and sat. She sat opposite.

"It was obvious, Stone. She was coming back for you. I waited for her outside."

"How was that obvious?"

"She was in love with you. Don't tell me you didn't see that. I saw it straightaway."

"How could she be in love with me? She was crazy!"

"What? Crazy people can't fall in love?"

I had no answer for that, so I ate and drank my coffee. I frowned. "How could you have seen it from the start? You didn't see her till today." She raised an eyebrow at me. "What? Don't give me that look. How could you have seen that?"

"Shut up and eat your eggs."

We ate in silence for a bit. Then, I said, "If you were waiting outside, why did you take so long?"

She looked sheepish. "I fell asleep. When I woke up, her car was there."

"You fell *asleep*?"

"Gimme a break! I was tired. I got here, didn't I?"

We ate in silence again for a while. Then, she grinned and said, "So, a week off, huh?"

"He said a few days."

"A week."

"Okay."

"What do you want to do?"

"I read an article in the *New York Times* the other day, said there is a steak house up in Maine that serves the best steaks on the East Coast. Family-run joint, on the quay, in a small town called Kennebunkport."

"Got to be worth it just for the name, right?"

"Right. I thought a few days relaxing by the sea, eat a few steaks, drink a few beers."

"A few tequilas."

"Rude not to."

"Set off after lunch?"

"Sounds about right."

Don't miss THE SINS OF THE FATHER. The riveting sequel in the Dead Cold Mystery series.

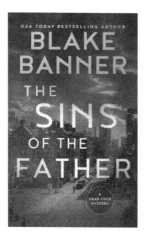

Scan the QR code below to purchase THE SINS OF THE FATHER.

Or go to: righthouse.com/the-sins-of-the-father

NOTE: flip to the very end to read an exclusive sneak peak...

DON'T MISS ANYTHING!

If you want to stay up to date on all new releases in this series, with this author, or with any of our new deals, you can do so by joining our newsletters below.

In addition, you will immediately gain access to our entire *Right House VIP Library*, which includes many riveting Mystery and Thriller novels for your enjoyment!

righthouse.com/email

(Easy to unsubscribe. No spam. Ever.)

ALSO BY BLAKE BANNER

Up to date books can be found at:
www.righthouse.com/blake-banner

ROGUE THRILLERS
Gates of Hell (Book 1)
Hell's Fury (Book 2)

ALEX MASON THRILLERS
Odin (Book 1)
Ice Cold Spy (Book 2)
Mason's Law (Book 3)
Assets and Liabilities (Book 4)
Russian Roulette (Book 5)
Executive Order (Book 6)
Dead Man Talking (Book 7)
All The King's Men (Book 8)
Flashpoint (Book 9)
Brotherhood of the Goat (Book 10)
Dead Hot (Book 11)
Blood on Megiddo (Book 12)
Son of Hell (Book 13)

HARRY BAUER THRILLER SERIES
Dead of Night (Book 1)
Dying Breath (Book 2)
The Einstaat Brief (Book 3)
Quantum Kill (Book 4)
Immortal Hate (Book 5)
The Silent Blade (Book 6)
LA: Wild Justice (Book 7)

Breath of Hell (Book 8)
Invisible Evil (Book 9)
The Shadow of Ukupacha (Book 10)
Sweet Razor Cut (Book 11)
Blood of the Innocent (Book 12)
Blood on Balthazar (Book 13)
Simple Kill (Book 14)
Riding The Devil (Book 15)
The Unavenged (Book 16)
The Devil's Vengeance (Book 17)
Bloody Retribution (Book 18)
Rogue Kill (Book 19)
Blood for Blood (Book 20)

DEAD COLD MYSTERY SERIES

An Ace and a Pair (Book 1)
Two Bare Arms (Book 2)
Garden of the Damned (Book 3)
Let Us Prey (Book 4)
The Sins of the Father (Book 5)
Strange and Sinister Path (Book 6)
The Heart to Kill (Book 7)
Unnatural Murder (Book 8)
Fire from Heaven (Book 9)
To Kill Upon A Kiss (Book 10)
Murder Most Scottish (Book 11)
The Butcher of Whitechapel (Book 12)
Little Dead Riding Hood (Book 13)
Trick or Treat (Book 14)
Blood Into Wine (Book 15)
Jack In The Box (Book 16)
The Fall Moon (Book 17)
Blood In Babylon (Book 18)
Death In Dexter (Book 19)
Mustang Sally (Book 20)

ABOUT US

Right House is an independent publisher created by authors for readers. We specialize in Action, Thriller, Mystery, and Crime novels.

If you enjoyed this novel, then there is a good chance you will like what else we have to offer! Please stay up to date by using any of the links below.

Join our mailing lists to stay up to date --> righthouse.com/email
Visit our website --> righthouse.com
Contact us --> contact@righthouse.com

 facebook.com/righthousebooks
x.com/righthousebooks
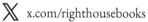 instagram.com/righthousebooks

EXCLUSIVE SNEAK PEAK OF...

SINS OF THE FATHER

CHAPTER 1

"This one."

She had her boots crossed on the corner of the desk, at the end of her mile-long legs, and she was leaning back in a pool of lazy September sunshine. She threw the file she had been reading on the desk in front of me.

I sighed and dropped the one I'd been reading—a disemboweled mob lawyer—into the "maybe later" pile and picked up her folder from the desk. She closed her eyes and made a temple of her fingers, as though she were Sherlock Holmes. I was struck, not for the first or last time, by how exquisite her face was. She opened one eye and raised that eyebrow at me. "Are you going to read it?"

I sat back and put my ankles on the desk next to hers.

"Simon Martin, thirty-two, beaten and stabbed during a home invasion on the fifth of September, 1999, Bogart Avenue. That's not far from here. Victim had just got home from work. He had bruising to the ribs and a jaw break consistent with having been punched, and he had been stabbed in the chest with a very large knife. Weapon was *not* found. Wife, Sylvie, was apparently upstairs at the time of the assault, but suffered shock-induced amnesia, so was unable to give a statement . . ." I gave Dehan a skeptical glance, but her eyes were still closed. I continued. "There were no signs of forced entry. The back door was unlocked, and there were footprints in the garden from common white tennis shoes, size ten or eleven. You awake?"

"I'm listening."

"You can't look and listen at the same time? I thought women were supposed to be good at multitasking."

She opened her eyes and revealed a total lack of humor. "Really, Stone? Sexist stereotyping, now, are we? That is so typical of a man. The more sensory input you can shut down, the more you are able to focus."

I ignored her and looked back at the file, glancing through the pages. "Okay. Yeah, let's do it."

"You're not going to read the rest of the file?"

"Tell me about it as we go."

As we stepped out into the early afternoon, she said, "You know, Stone, you are not an unattractive man."

I frowned at her. We crossed the road toward my burgundy 1964 Jaguar Mark II and I thought absently that it was not an unattractive car.

Dehan continued, which was a little unsettling. "You are not unlike the man, Bogart."

"Knock it awf, shweetheart."

I unlocked the car and climbed in.

As she got in the passenger seat, she said, "I'm serious. You're taller—what are you, six two?"

"Six one."

"Perhaps Harrison Ford or Hugh Jackman would be a better comparison."

I reversed out of the lot and pulled onto Storey Avenue, headed east. I settled back in my seat and scowled. "Dehan," I said with a degree of severity. "I know what you are doing. The answer is no, I do not want a woman in my life. What is it with you and trying to get me paired up?"

"I don't know, Stone. You're a good-looking guy, you're comparatively young . . ."

"Thanks."

"You're one of the good guys, and believe me, that is *rare*. It just seems like a waste that you are single. It's a shame."

"We have had this conversation before. And besides, I could say the same about you. Only you are not a good-looking guy. You are . . ." I waved my hand around, realizing the conversation was getting into dangerous waters. "Anyway, the fact is we would probably both make terrible husbands and wives."

She shrugged. "You would be a terrible wife. I would probably be a pretty good husband."

"You are a very disturbing woman."

She sighed. "That is what my shrink keeps telling me."

I took Rosedale North as far as East Tremont, then turned left onto Bronxdale and right onto Pierce. Bogart was the second on the left. I parked outside the Martins' house and looked at Dehan. She seemed abstracted. I smiled. "I'm glad it was Bogart Avenue and not Karloff."

She gave a sad smile and climbed out.

There was a fish sticker in the window that told me that Jesus loved me. Another one told me that even though I did not believe in God, God believed in me. I was pretty sure they were both wrong. Dehan came up beside me and commented, "If they keep putting up enlightening stickers, they are going to block out the light."

"Droll."

I rang the bell and knocked on the door. Almost like a weird coincidence, the neighbor's door opened, and a woman with a very large, nosy air about her looked at me like she wanted to accuse me of something but didn't know what yet.

"They ain't in."

I smiled the smile of an innocent man and said, "Where are they?"

"Church. They are always at church."

I nodded. "Of course. Can you tell me where the church is?"

She smiled unexpectedly and looked a hundred years younger.

"Out back." She pointed, in case I didn't know where out back was. "Fowler Avenue. Right at the back, here . . . You can walk it."

I thanked her again, and we descended the steps we had recently just climbed up. It was a three-hundred-yard stroll through an odd neighborhood that blended leafy trees in the first russet shades of fall with very homey redbrick houses and soulless concrete yards fenced with steel tubing and wire mesh. The overall vibe was a very unhappy one.

The church was small and, judging by the design, early-twentieth-century Methodist. It was a sturdy redbrick building with towering Gothic arches and a rotund tower at the very back. It stood in its own grounds, surrounded by towering maple trees and gloomy-looking chestnut trees. There was a cute redbrick rectory on the left. The door, which stood open, was now dull, but once must have been a vibrant red, with a set of heavy, black iron hinges. A flagged path led to a small graveyard on the right, and beyond that there was a large garden. There, some kind of church fête seemed to be in progress. There was bunting strung from the trees, and there were stalls selling secondhand clothes, books, vinyl records, record players, and old rusty tools, as well as homemade lemonade, chocolate brownies, cookies, and cakes. There was a big crowd swirling around the church grounds.

We strolled in among the throng of people and headed for the cake stall. It was attended by a pretty, blond woman who must have been in her late thirties, and a pretty girl who had to be her daughter stood beside her. She was probably in her late teens or early twenties. They both gave us bright smiles that looked as though they belonged in the South, where life was good and morality was uncomplicated.

"Hi there!" It was the woman. She said it like we were old friends, and for a moment I wondered if I knew her. "Welcome! Can we offer you some amazing lemonade?"

Dehan answered before I could draw breath. "You sure can, and we'll have a couple of those brownies too."

The daughter poured while the mother shoveled. I took my

brownie from her and said, "Maybe you can help us. We are actually looking for somebody."

"Oh." She seemed genuinely pleased at the possibility of being able to help. "Well, we know most everyone around here, don't we, honey?"

Her daughter nodded and also looked equally as eager to help. Dehan said, "Sylvie Martin?"

They were thrilled, and I swear the mother gave a little jump. "Oh, well, that's me! I am Sylvie Martin!" She took hold of her daughter and added, "And this is Mary, my daughter! How can we help you?"

Dehan's mouth was full of chocolate brownie, so all she could say was, "Umph . . ."

I took over, with what is generally termed as "an easy smile." "We are police officers." I put down my lemonade, fished out my badge, and showed it to her. "I am Detective John Stone, and this is my partner, Detective Carmen Dehan."

A hint of a frown, the smile strained almost imperceptibly by concern as soon as the words "police officer" hit her ears.

"Oh, is there a problem . . . ?"

"No." I shook my head and bit into the brownie. It was good, and I allowed my face to say so. Speaking with my mouth full, I said, "It is the policy of the Forty-Third Precinct to review cold cases from time to time, Mrs. Martin, and we are currently conducting a review of . . ."

I trailed off. She had gone very pale. Her daughter was watching her and had placed her hand on her shoulder. Sylvie said, "I thought that was a permanently closed case."

Dehan swallowed the last of her brownie and said, "Simon's murderer is still at large, Sylvie. The case can't be closed."

"I would . . . We would all, really, rather put the whole thing behind us. The Lord dispenses His own justice."

"I'm sorry, Mrs. Martin." I meant it; she looked genuinely distressed. "But we have to do our job. Is there somewhere we can talk privately?"

She gave a deep sigh and searched the crowd for a moment. Then she raised a hand and called, "Oh, Paul . . . Reverend Truelove . . . !"

I turned and watched a large, leonine man, with silver hair swept back from his head in a perfect swoop, move through the crowd toward us. He looked for a moment like a Spanish galleon parting the seas in some forgotten, surrealist book of the Old Testament. He graced us both with the bounty of his kind smile, lingering a little longer and with more bounty upon the beautiful Dehan than on me. Finally, he turned to Sylvie Martin.

"Sylvie, who are your friends?" Then, turning to us again, he said, "Welcome to St. George's." He had a voice like a particularly excellent church organ.

I showed him my badge. "Detectives Stone and Dehan, NYPD. Superb brownies and lemonade, by the way. We were wondering if we could borrow Sylvie for five minutes. It is purely a formality. We are reviewing a cold case . . ."

He frowned. "A cold case? You can't mean poor Simon, surely?"

Dehan, with her usual directness, asked, "Why not?"

"Well." He smiled. "That must be sixteen or seventeen years ago."

"Eighteen, but it is still unsolved." She grinned. "So we keep working at solving it until we bring him justice."

"I see." He frowned as though he did not agree. "Well, that is very commendable. By all means, would you like to use the vestry?" He gestured with his hand, ushering us in that direction. Turning to Sylvie's daughter, he said, "Mary, you'll tend the stall for a moment, won't you?"

She smiled. "Of course, Reverend."

Sylvie Martin led us down the side of the church, under the shadow of the trees, toward the side door into the nave, and all the way I could feel Reverend Paul Truelove's eyes burning on my back.

CHAPTER 2

THE INSIDE OF THE CHURCH WAS DARK BY CONTRAST with the bright sunshine outside. The Gothic arch of the doorway, on the far right, was startling, luminous in red and green. And on the left, there was the tenuous flicker of candles by the altar. Sylvie crossed herself and led us from the transept to another perfectly arched, wooden door that gave on to the vestry at the back of the altar.

We followed her into a comfortable room that had the feel of an old-world library or study. There was an oak desk, a two-seater sofa, and a couple of black leather chairs. Two tall, frosted windows looked out onto the colorful fête outside. Sylvie sat on the sofa with her knees together and bent them slightly to one side. Dehan and I took the chairs. I smiled in a way I hoped was reassuring.

"Mrs. Martin . . ."

"Sylvie, please."

"Sylvie. We understand that this must be difficult, and the last thing we want to do is stir up any painful memories. But you understand, a serious crime has been committed, and we are obliged to investigate."

She nodded. "Yes, of course I understand. I will try to help in any way that I can, I mean if I can . . ."

"What can you tell us about the events of that evening?"

She placed her hands, one on top of the other, on her lap and looked at them sadly, as though they had disappointed her somehow.

"My memory . . ." she said. "My memory of that evening is practically nonexistent, if I am being honest. I just seemed to black out at the time, and it has never come back."

Dehan said, "Don't worry. Don't force yourself. How about the hour or two before?"

She smiled briefly at Dehan and said, "Um . . . I had fed and changed Mary. She was just one at the time. Ahmed had come over from the church . . ."

"Ahmed?"

"He was a refugee, a young Arab boy, from Iraq. He was just sixteen, and Paul—that's Reverend Truelove—had offered him some work at the church to give him a hand in making ends meet. Odd jobs, gardening and whatnot. We all hoped he would find the true faith, but we never pressured him."

I frowned. "And he had come over to your house?"

"Simon had offered him work too, in the garden, a few afternoons a week."

Dehan sat forward. "So you had fed and changed Mary, and then Ahmed had come over and he was working in the garden."

"Yes . . ."

"What happened next?"

Her face seemed to go tight. Her fingers closed on the hem of her dress. "I suppose it must have gotten dark. I am not sure. I know Simon came home from work. I remember he was calling to say he was home, but none of the lights were on in the house. I hate to waste electricity, you see, but I remember that the kitchen door out into the garden was open. I remember that without a doubt. I know I was sitting on the bottom of the stairs and the house was completely dark and still. I felt a bit cold. And Simon was lying there, in his coat. His briefcase was next to him and he was staring straight up at the ceiling."

She frowned, as though she was trying to remember something, and I was surprised to realize she was crying. She held her breath for a moment, and suddenly she was like a woman with a bad cold. I reached over and handed her my handkerchief, and Dehan moved and sat next to her, putting her arm around her shoulders.

"Where was Ahmed?"

"Gone. Gone before the dusk."

"I know it is hard, but please try to remember. Did anybody else call?"

"I don't know. The kitchen door was open, into the garden."

I smiled at her. "Do you come from Texas?"

She gave a small, damp laugh. "Is it that obvious?"

"Y'all still got the twang."

She laughed and wagged a finger at me. "Y'all ain't never singular, Detective Stone. Y'all best remember that!" She fiddled with the handkerchief for a moment, then said, "Simon worked at Federal United. They transferred him here. We didn't really want to leave Austin, we liked it there, but it was a chance for a promotion and more money . . ." She shrugged. "So we took it. We could have gone to Brooklyn. The bank offered us a place there. But Simon said we could do more good through the church here, where there was more need."

For a moment, I was reminded of the stickers in her window, but I didn't mention them. Instead, I asked her, "Who alerted the police?"

She stared at me. It was an odd expression, almost apologetic. "I had the phone in my hand . . . It must have been me."

Dehan stroked her back a couple of times. "Did you speak to him?" Sylvie turned to look at her. Dehan went on, "He called to you to let you know he was home. Did you answer? Did you say anything?"

Her bottom lip began to quiver. She made a strange, guttural sound like, "Oh, God . . . !" and collapsed against her, sobbing. Dehan enfolded her in her arms and looked at me, shaking her head.

I sat for a moment, watching her and thinking. When she had settled a bit, I said, "We won't trouble you any more today, Sylvie, but we may want to talk to you again as the investigation progresses. I do understand it's hard, but I would like you to give some thought to Detective Dehan's questions and see if anything begins to surface in your memory. Can you do that for me?"

She nodded, blinking, and blew her nose. "I'm sorry."

I stood. "No need to be at all."

"I suppose I had better get back to my daughter."

I smiled. "Y'all take care, y'hear?"

She laughed sadly and we followed her out into the nave. As we approached the transept, a shadow moved across the door at the far end, and a foot seemed to scuff the stone floor, setting up an echo in the vaulted ceiling. Sylvie stopped and peered, and blew her nose.

"Humberto?" The figure shuffled closer. Dehan glanced at me. Sylvie said again, "Humberto, is that you?"

He was tall, almost seven feet, and massive, though he stooped and had a shambling gait. Slowly, he came into the diffuse light of the candles. His features were hard to make out with the glare of sunlight behind him, but his face was broad, his jaw was big, and his brow was low on his face. He was grinning as he came closer. Both his grin and his steps were hesitant. When he spoke, his voice was nasally.

"*Donna Maria, benedicta santisima, purisima mater nostra . . .*" He laughed nervously, making a sound like a braying ass, knocked his knees, and gripped his crotch with both hands. "*Perdonattame, perdonattame . . .*"

She smiled at him. "It's okay, Humberto, you can sit and pray, *orare, orare,* you can sit."

He brayed again, biting his lower lip. "*Santisima madre, benedita, plena di grattia . . .*"

He backed away and after a couple of steps turned and dashed off into the shadows among the rear pews. Sylvie opened the side door at the end of the transept and we stepped out into the sunshine. Dehan asked it. She had to, and I knew it was killing her to know.

"Who is that?"

"Humberto?" Sylvie shrugged. "He's attached to Paul . . ." She sighed. "Sorry, Reverend Truelove. Nobody really knows his story. He just seems always to have been here. I suspect the reverend adopted him at some point, but he's so humble, he never talks about it." She shrugged. "Either way, he has found a home, literally, in the church."

I frowned. "What is that language he speaks? It's not Latin or Italian."

She laughed. "It is some kind of peculiar invention of his own. It's a generic Latin. People have identified Portuguese, Italian, Spanish, modern Latin, and classical Latin, plus a good few inventions of his own. He seems to make it up as he goes along."

"How old is he?"

She shrugged and shook her head. "Nobody knows."

I saw the reverend walking toward us. Sylvie held up the handkerchief. "I will wash it and return it to you when you are around next. Thank you for being so understanding. I'd better go."

She had taken less than a dozen paces when she and the reverend crossed. We watched as he stopped and took hold of her shoulders. They looked into each other's faces but they did not speak. After a moment, he patted her on the arm and she moved off in the direction of her stall, and Reverend Truelove—Paul— approached us with the walk of a man who owns a God who owns the world.

Without preamble, he said, "It was almost two decades ago, but to her it's as raw and livid as though it had happened today, five minutes ago."

"The mind is its own place, reverend, and can make a heaven of hell, a hell of heaven."

He looked at me curiously. "Indeed. Was she able to help any? It was a long time ago. Memories fade . . ."

Dehan scratched her head. "Well, Reverend, from what you just said, it was a long time ago for you, but not for her. So her memory hasn't faded." She affected the accent of the Deep South. "The mind bein' its own place, an' all." She pointed at the large group of people milling among the stalls. There were perhaps eighty or a hundred of them. "See those people, Reverend? How many of them do you reckon were here eighteen years ago?"

He looked startled. "I am not sure. Most of them, I should think."

"And how many of them, would you say, knew for sure that Sylvie's kitchen door was open that evening?"

His jaw dropped and he stared at her in astonishment.

She plowed on. "Because, Reverend, in that—much smaller—group, you will probably find a man who wanted to kill Simon Martin." She smiled. "Kind of changes things, doesn't it? Bit less vague and a bit more immediate."

He did the goldfish thing of staring with big eyes and soundlessly opening and closing his mouth.

I smiled at him and asked, "Were you here that evening, Reverend?"

"Why . . . yes, um, I'm not sure . . . No." He shook his head. "I truly don't recall."

I shrugged. "It's a long time ago. I just thought, given the events of the night . . ."

"Oh, quite so. It just escapes my mind at the moment. I can tell you that I didn't find out what had happened until the next morning. But for the life of me . . ." He hesitated. "It was a terrible shock, of course. I felt somehow guilty that I hadn't been here for her at the time . . ."

I nodded, then gave a small, sideways twitch of my head. "You can hardly be held responsible for that. What kind of man was Simon? Do you know of any enemies he might have had?"

He puffed out his cheeks. "It is hard to imagine such a thing. He was a committed Christian, and a genuinely good man." He gave a knowing smile, inviting us to join him in a cozy joke. "Because, as we know, there are many committed Christians, who are not necessarily genuinely good people."

Dehan snorted. "You got that right."

He raised an eyebrow at her that said he found her vaguely distasteful, then addressed me. "He was a serious man, did not invite easy friendship, but he was very upright and did a great deal for charity, and for the church."

I scratched my chin. "I have to ask this, Reverend, and I hope you understand that there is nothing to be gained by concealing the truth through a misguided sense of loyalty." He looked affronted, but I ignored him and carried on. "How were things at home between Simon and Sylvie?"

He looked grave. "To be honest, a little joyless. Simon was a very devout man who saw little point in having fun. Joy, in his view, was to be achieved exclusively through an undivided devotion to God." He sighed and spread his hands. "Sylvie is a joyful, happy soul, and I fear she was withering a little in their marriage." He smiled beatifically. "Of course, Mary brought her much joy and laughter while Simon was at work, but, well, their life together was serious and contemplative, rather than gay and exuberant." He smiled thinly at Dehan. "I use the word gay in its true meaning, of course."

I nodded. "Would you have described Sylvie as frustrated back then?"

He looked uncomfortable. "I don't know that I would have chosen *that* particular word, but let's say I would not have described her as *fulfilled*. However, certainly not frustrated to the point of *homicide*, if that is what you are getting at."

I shook my head. "I am not driving at anything, Reverend,

just trying to understand the situation. We have no suspects yet at this time, unfortunately."

Dehan frowned. "One last question and then we'll leave you in peace . . . for a bit. Does Sylvie have a job . . . ?" She shrugged, shook her head, and spread her hands all at the same time. "What is her source of income?"

"Simon had made a very generous cushion, if you will, for her by means of a couple of insurance policies. That was him all over. So she works full time, on a voluntary basis, at the church. To be working in God's service helps her to heal from what happened so many years ago."

I held out my hand. "Thank you, Reverend. We'll try not to disturb you unnecessarily, but we will need to talk to you again at some point during this investigation."

He took my hand in both of his and held it tight. "Well, naturally, any help we can offer you, we will be only too glad to assist. But I have to say, Detective, it has taken Sylvie a long time to get back on her feet. We have all been there for her, to help and support her through very dark times. It would be a shame if, in seeking Simon's killer, you reopened wounds that are only just beginning to heal."

"I hear you, Reverend. We will be as sensitive as we can."

We shook hands and made our way back to the car.

CHAPTER 3

INSTEAD OF GOING BACK TO THE PRECINCT, I TURNED right on Van Nest and then left onto Paulding and pulled up in front of Doyle's Pub. We grabbed a couple of beers and went to sit at a small table by the window. Dehan started talking while I took a pull and wiped the froth from my mouth.

"Okay, brief review of the facts: Sylvie is home alone with her newborn, Mary. The kid, Ahmed, is out in the garden doing the gardening. Neighbors—and you would know this if you had read the file—reported that they saw Simon arrive home in his car shortly after seven."

She paused to drink, smacked her lips, and sighed. I interrupted her.

"He lets himself in and finds that the lights are off. She made a point of that and she is not there to greet him. He was the kind of man, I suspect, who would have expected his wife to be there to greet him, with his dinner ready. But she said she heard him calling out for her."

"So why were the lights off and . . ."

I pulled a face. "I don't like 'why.' It is too open. What was it that stopped her from putting on the lights, as she would normally have done? Focuses the question a lot more keenly. What was it that stopped her from being at the door when he arrived? I wonder if there was a meal being cooked . . ."

"You done, Sensei?"

I nodded.

"So, something unusual has happened *before* Simon gets home that has prevented his good wife from preparing for his homecoming." She raised a finger. "Now, things happen pretty quick at this point. Simon is struck forcefully in the ribs and on the jaw. The medic's report says he was bruised, premortem, on his left floating ribs and on the left side of his mandible. Which may have caused him to collapse on the floor. He was found still wearing his coat, stabbed in the chest, and, as Sylvie said, with his briefcase still by his side. All of which suggests he was barely through the door when he was attacked and murdered."

"You said stabbed in the chest, not stabbed in the heart."

"Yes. He was stabbed right through the sternum, at the height of the third intercostals."

"Through the sternum? You're sure?"

She raised an eyebrow. "What do you think? You think I'm sure?"

"I think you're sure."

"The blow must have been delivered with considerable force, which adds weight to the theory that he was lying on his back at the time he was stabbed. So his assailant was able to put all their weight behind the knife."

"Okay, so the picture suggests that the killer was the unknown element that prevented Sylvie from putting on the lights and dutifully greeting Simon at the door. And as soon as he came in, the killer struck. The position of the body was, if I am not mistaken, at the foot of the stairs . . ."

"Correct, which would suggest that the killer was either on the stairs or up the stairs when Simon came in the door."

"And from what Sylvie has told us, she was found sitting on

the stairs, with the telephone in her hands. The actions around the trauma all center around the stairs."

Dehan nodded. "The 911 call was made from the phone she was holding."

I stared at the dry rings on the mahogany tabletop, seeing my imagined version of the Martins' entrance hall. "So the idea is that Sylvie is being held upstairs by the killer. Simon comes home, calls her, and the killer rushes down, punches him twice with his right fist, first in the ribs and then on the jaw, and, when he falls to the ground, he sits on him and stabs him through the sternum." I frowned at Dehan. "How many stab wounds?"

She smiled. "I was wondering when you'd ask that. Two."

"Hmmm . . . So our killer is in a bit of a frenzy and is certainly not a seasoned assassin. He has delivered two blows where one would have been ample, and he has stabbed him in the most difficult place on the chest. While, presumably, Sylvie is standing on the stairs watching him. It is very odd."

She turned her glass around a few times on the table, like she was trying to screw it down, or wind it up. After a moment, she said, "You're not wrong. I keep asking myself, 'Where was the phone?'"

She looked up at me and I nodded. It was what I had been asking myself too.

She went on, "What did she do? Stand there and watch her husband get murdered, then go to fetch the phone and return to sit on the stairs to call 911?"

I pulled a face, like I knew I wasn't convincing her and I wasn't really convincing myself either. "Maybe it was upstairs."

She echoed my expression with a shrug. "Maybe. Same thing applies. Anyway, motive and opportunity: prima facie . . ."

I smiled. "I like that. That's good. Prima facie. It's nice."

"You like that? It's good, huh? Thank you. So, prima facie, the only motive we can be sure of is Sylvie's."

"The life insurance."

"It has got to be pretty generous because it is paying either for the rent on a substantial house, or the mortgage. Plus, it's giving her enough to live on without having to work. If, on top of that, he was a miserable bastard to be married to . . ."

"That is a big assumption, Dehan."

She offered me a smile that was richer in scorn than in mirth. "Come on! He saw 'little point in fun,' and 'joy was to be achieved exclusively through devotion to God.' I call that being a miserable bastard. And remember . . ." She wagged a finger at me. "For a woman like Sylvie, divorce is not an option. The vow is 'till death do us part,' and God holds them to that. The penalty is not just hell, but being ostracized by their community. Hell is just an imagined future. Being reviled and ostracized is a hard reality to live with, especially for someone like Sylvie."

"So she was stuck with him for life."

"For the next sixty years."

"Unless . . ."

"Unless he died before that. Drink up. The next ones are on me."

"I have to drive."

"We are a ten-minute walk from your house. We'll be having spaghetti tonight."

"We are? Okay, sounds great to me."

I watched the streetlights come on through the darkening glass in the windows, and the attitude of people's walk shift from a businesslike stride to a homeward hurry as evening enclosed around them, past parking cars with amber headlamps. I thought of Sylvie, curled helpless against Dehan's shoulder, weeping, hiding from the truth in the shadows of amnesia.

Dehan sat and placed a glass in front of me. "I know what you're going to say," she said. "Sylvie hasn't the strength, either physical or of character, to knock her husband to the ground and stab him twice through the sternum. And I would have to agree. But that doesn't take away the fact that, so far, she is the only person with an apparent motive."

I took another pull on the beer. "So are we talking about an accomplice? That would imply a second motive."

"Do you ever wish you smoked, Stone?"

"Sometimes."

"Right now I could definitely use a cigarette."

"I read that nicotine helps ward off Alzheimer's."

"He didn't actually have the disease. It wasn't his."

"No, he just discovered it."

"So, who else stood to gain by Simon's death, Stone? The kid, Mary, was only about one year old. Reverend Paul Truelove?"

"Love? Sex? If that's the case, why haven't they gotten together since?"

She shrugged and sipped, then shrugged again as she put down the glass. "Maybe her Christian guilt kicked in and she repented after the deed was done. But we might equally ask, how come she hasn't gone back to Texas? Remember, Reverend Truelove was keen for us not to pursue the investigation because, and I quote, she was 'healing, working for God.'"

"Good points all three. Plus, he has no alibi for the night in question. Still, this is mere surmise at this stage; we need hard evidence to make it stick."

"I will contact her insurance company tomorrow and see how big the payout was."

I turned it over a few times in my mind with my glass halfway to my mouth. I spoke absently, half to myself, "I want to talk to the first emergency responders too. I'm interested in the wound. It might have more to tell us . . ."

Walking toward my house about half an hour later, through quiet, lamplit streets, Dehan said, "I guess if either one of us was in a relationship, we couldn't do this anymore, huh?"

I looked at her with big eyes. "Do what?"

"I mean, me stay over in your guest room, have dinner and breakfast . . . A husband or a wife would make that kind of hard."

I gave a small laugh. "Are you brooding, Dehan? What's eating you today?"

"Nothing! I'm just wondering. Jeez . . . I'm Jewish already! We overthink everything. It's part of our purpose in the world. Other people don't think enough, so we overthink to compensate . . ."

"You're babbling again."

"We do that too."

"Are you trying to tell me you met someone?"

"No!"

The expression of horror on her face made me laugh. "It's okay if you did, it's cool. Everything is cool."

She spoke to her boots. "I just keep wondering why you haven't."

THINGS DIDN'T GO EXACTLY as planned the next morning. As I sat down behind my desk at eight a.m., my phone rang.

"Stone."

I saw Dehan roll her eyes and frown-shrugged "what?" at her. She made a face like a gorilla answering the phone and mouthed, "Stone!"

I turned away because Reverend Paul Truelove was talking to me.

"Ah, Detective Stone, I am glad to catch you early. I was wondering if I might come in and have a chat with you."

"Of course. What's it about?"

"So, would half an hour suit you?"

"Just fine. See you then."

Dehan was typing. She said, "Who?" to the screen.

"Reverend Truelove. Wants to have a chat in half an hour. He's on his way already, apparently."

She smiled and raised an eyebrow. "Hmmm . . ."

"What are you doing?"

She picked up her phone and dialed. "Insurance." She stood up and walked away on very long, slim legs. I called Frank.

"Hey, Frank, Stone here. How is it hanging?"

"Loose. What can I do for you?"

"Fifth September, 1999. Simon Martin. Stabbed through the sternum, twice, does that ring any bells?"

His laugh was mirthless. "You know how many stabbings we've had in the last eighteen years, Stone?"

"No. Can you look it up? Maybe even scare up the pathologist who did the report by this afternoon?"

"Yes, maybe, no. Yes, I can look it up. Maybe I can scare up the pathologist if he, she, or it is still in a condition to be scared. No, I can't do it by this afternoon. I'll call you when I have looked into it."

"I appreciate it."

"No, you don't. You take me for granted."

"You're right. I do, I'm sorry."

He hung up.

Dehan was strolling back across the room, listening carefully to her cell. She spoke briefly, giving her email address. Then she sat, hung up, and reached behind her head to tie her hair in a knot at the back of her neck.

"He had two insurance policies. The first covered the mortgage on the house in the event of his death. Which means that she basically got the house without having to pay for it. The second gave her an income for life of five thousand dollars a month; so sixty grand a year."

"Holy cow. That's like having a million bucks in the bank and living off the interest."

She leaned back in her chair and picked up a pencil, which she put in her mouth as though it were a cheroot. "I have a perfect life. The only problem is this pain in the ass of a husband who keeps pissing on my parade. Now, to make matters worse, he has taken out two insurance policies that make him totally redundant."

I thought for a moment and wagged a finger at her. "We need to take a closer look at the nature of those bruises. Frank is looking up the case. He's going to get back to me." I checked my watch. "Let's grab some coffee before the reverend gets here."

Scan the QR code below to purchase THE SINS OF THE FATHER.
Or go to: righthouse.com/the-sins-of-the-father

Made in the USA
Las Vegas, NV
01 March 2025

18905663R00127